BECAUSE WE LOVED

A CHRISTIAN ROMANCE

JULIETTE DUNCAN

TRANSFORMED BY LOVE SERIES - BOOK 1

Cover Design by http://www.StunningBookCovers.com

Copyright © 2019 Juliette Duncan

All rights reserved.

THE HOLY BIBLE, NEW INTERNATIONAL VERSION®, NIV® Copyright © 1973, 1978, 1984, 2011 by Biblica, Inc.™ Used by permission. All rights reserved worldwide.

PRAISE FOR "BECAUSE WE LOVED"

"This is my favorite of Juliette Duncan's books that I've had the pleasure to read. They're all good, but I just absolutely loved this one. I enjoyed reading about Callum and Fleur's romance, about Callum's coming to faith, and about Fleur's living out her faith. There were several serious issues addressed--losing men in battle, PTSD, grieving a spouse, not dating an unbeliever; and yet, the book is uplifting and encouraging. I highly recommend it to readers of clean/wholesome romance and to Christian romance readers." ~LGS

"This is the first military love story that I have read and it didn't disappoint. Juliette Duncan is a masterful storyteller and the characters always seem so real that they could be your neighbors. I love how important issues like not dating an unbeliever, showing God's love in your actions, and PTSD are dealt with in a Godly manner. I highly recommend reading this book." ~Ann

"A beautifully written story rich with inspiration. The author does a wonderful job of using scripture that flows with the story. " ~Gina

FOREWORD

HELLO! Thank you for choosing to read this book - I hope you enjoy it! Please note that this story is set in Australia. Australian spelling and terminology have been used and are not typos!

As a thank you for reading this book, I'd like to offer you a FREE GIFT. That's right - my FREE novella, "Hank and Sarah - A Love Story" is available exclusively to my newsletter subscribers. Click here to claim your copy now and to be notified of my future book releases. I hope you enjoy both books! Have a wonderful day!

Juliette

PROLOGUE

*L*t Cl Westaway scanned the horizon, crouching low behind the scrubby hill. Creeping forward, he motioned with his hand for his men to follow. They needed the element of surprise. They'd spent days tracking this band of mujahideen, aiming to intercept them before they carried out their plans to cause more carnage in Kabul. These were dangerous and desperate men.

Callum blinked as a bead of sweat rolled down his forehead and onto his eyelashes. It was so hot, and the air, thick with dust, was almost tangible. A few metres away, flies buzzed nosily as they fed off a long dead goat.

He hated this place. Still, a few more days and it would be over. This was his last mission before a well-deserved leave. So far, things had gone according to plan, and none of his men had been lost, though one had been flown home wounded. Enough to put him out of active service for a while, but nothing fatal.

In fact, Callum had been thinking all morning that things had gone almost too well. He'd learned to take nothing for granted.

He breathed in slowly, a sudden sense of foreboding coming over him. Years in the field had honed his instincts, and he turned his head sharply to the right before he saw the figure running towards his men from seemingly nowhere, shouting a language he didn't speak, but whose words he recognised in their intent. The man's gun was raised in a fluid movement as he shouted commands to his men who followed.

It was too late. Callum's body lifted off the ground as a deafening explosion rang in his ears. As he dropped and rolled, his last image before he lost consciousness was Lt Jeff Gibbons a few yards away, staring at him with eyes that would never see again...

CALLUM WOKE WITH A GASP, his heart pounding inside his chest, his eyes wide in the darkened room.

It was a dream. Just a dream. I'm not there anymore.

Panting, he sat up and swung his legs over the side of the bed, deliberately slowing and lengthening his breath. There was no need to panic. He was safe.

As he thought it, his insides twisted with shame. Since when did Lt Cl Westaway worry about being safe? While far from reckless—recklessness had no place in the field—he had a reputation for both bravery and stoicism in the face of conflict. Never in all his years of active duty had he felt the need to reassure himself he was 'safe'.

He hadn't had these dreams until recently, since returning to his base at Salford after an active tour in the Middle East. After years in the field and a distinguished and decorated career, he'd succumbed to the lure of the desk job.

Well, sort of. He was due to start his new job the following day, training new recruits at Salford Barracks, and while he was satisfied that he'd made the right decision, he was conflicted about it. An old adage of his father's 'those who can, do; those who can't, teach' kept coming back to him. It was nonsense, of course. Callum had proved himself in the field enough times. At thirty-eight, it was time to take a step back, and Salford was delighted to have him as a Senior Trainer, believing he would be an ideal model for eager new recruits. He just hoped he could live up to their expectations. He'd had little teaching experience and if he was honest with himself, he was anxious about the day ahead, probably the reason for having the dreams. Nerves.

He padded across the room in his bare feet and downstairs to the kitchen. The three-bedroom town house he lived in, courtesy of the Defence Force, was lovely but often felt too big for him alone. He had plans to turn the spare bedrooms into a study and a gym but hadn't made a start on them yet. Maybe he wasn't ready to resign himself to a life alone, although he couldn't fathom anything else.

He'd been single since he and Danielle had divorced years earlier. Childhood sweethearts, it had never occurred to him they wouldn't have children and stay together forever. But after only three years of marriage, she'd announced she was leaving, that being an army wife wasn't for her, particularly after her friend's husband had been killed in active duty. He'd been in shock for weeks, not believing it was true, expecting her to change her mind. He waited for the reconciliation letter that never came and resigned himself to the situation by the time the divorce papers arrived. It had been an amicable enough end, and he tried not to begrudge the fact that the last he'd heard of her, she was happily married with a baby on the way. Danielle deserved to be happy. He'd settled for busy and successful.

Any dream of a family to return to after a gruelling tour was put away in a box to gather dust. Only recently, since retiring from active duty, had he understood how lonely he really was. He'd lost too many good friends in the field to be keen to make new ones, and his parents lived miles away in Frankston. His father, a retired Colonel, had frowned on his decision to take the post at Salford.

Pushing thoughts of his overbearing father from his mind, he turned the kettle on. It was never too early in the morning for coffee. He set his focus on the day ahead, hoping it wouldn't bring with it too many surprises.

Maybe tomorrow night, he could sleep uninterrupted.

CHAPTER 1

SALFORD ARMY BASE, VICTORIA, AUSTRALIA

*C*allum stood at ease, listening to Colonel Jarrop run through his first day and what to expect. He tried to hide the fact that he was so tired. The man's monotonous voice was making him feel like going back to bed to catch up on missed sleep. After the nightmare, he'd stayed awake, and sitting on his balcony, had watched the sun come up. He'd seen the sun rise in many places during his army career, but had never paused long enough to take it in. Appreciate it. That morning, he'd witnessed the beauty of a summer sunrise in a clear sky and felt lucky to be alive.

So many weren't.

The pang of survivor's guilt had followed immediately after, spoiling his reverie. Often, his recent nightmares replayed scenes of friends and fellow soldiers dying in the field. Last night it had been Jeff Gibbons, a man who'd served under him in Afghanistan three years earlier. A pleasant guy, he was devoted to his wife and kids and talked about them constantly. Callum had still been a little raw over Danielle at that point and had tried not to feel envious of Jeff's fortune.

He'd thought of the family Gibbons had left behind a few times over the years and wondered how they were doing. He'd met his wife—Fleur, he thought her name was, it sounded like a flower—at the funeral. Even with her face twisted in grief, Callum had noticed her gentle but overwhelming beauty. He'd given her his condolences, but she'd looked through him, staring into a past she'd lost. Or perhaps a future she no longer recognised.

Seeing the Colonel staring at him quizzically, Callum pushed away his morbid thoughts. *What is wrong with me lately?* "Sorry sir, I didn't catch that."

The Colonel smiled genially. "I was just pointing out, West-away, after all of your experience in the field, dealing with a few new recruits should be child's play."

"I hope so, sir."

The Colonel rubbed his neck. "There's one recruit you may need to watch out for. Billy Cassidy. He's nineteen, I believe. He was on a fast track to prison until he decided to join the army and 'turn his life around.' A noble sentiment, but looking at his record, the boy's trouble."

Callum raised a brow. "But we've given him a chance?"

The Colonel nodded. "He shows promise. Passed all the entry tests with flying colours. Sometimes these boys are the ones who surpass all expectations and fly up the ranks. I guess because we give them a home and a purpose."

Callum smiled wryly. He could understand that. Despite his recent struggles, the army had been his home and purpose his entire adult life. "I'll keep an eye out for him. A few weeks of basic training will soon show what he's made of."

The Colonel looked pleased. "We're glad to have you, Westaway. Good luck."

Callum stood to attention, saluted and left the room. It was time to meet the recruits. His first class with them was Military History. He had them for Parade Training as well. At least he wasn't teaching PT. That would have annoyed his father.

THE MILITARY HISTORY class rapidly turned into what felt like his own biography as the recruits peppered him with questions after the lecture. Rather than asking him to tell them more about the history of the conflicts in the Middle East or the early days of the army, all they wanted to know about was Lt Cl Westaway.

"How many medals have you got?"

"How many tours have you been on?"

Callum laughed and answered their questions good-naturedly. While he knew it was important he retain his authority, he also knew their time at camp would be better supported by officers who seemed human, not just unapproachable seniors.

He was surprised by how much he was actually enjoying himself so far. Teaching seemed to suit him.

Billy Cassidy raised his hand. "I've got a question, sir." Callum nodded at him to continue. Contrary to the Colonel's warnings, Billy had been no trouble whatsoever. In fact, he seemed happy to be there and eager to learn. Apparently he'd excelled in PT. Looking at his lean but wiry frame, Callum wasn't surprised.

"Have you seen a lot of death?" the youth asked.

Callum blinked. Was this lad somehow reading his mind? Were his night terrors on show for all to see? Clearing his throat, he answered more brusquely than he'd intended, "Of course, Cassidy. In war, people die."

There were a few nervous titters, but most of the recruits went quiet and looked at him intently. How many of them grasped the realities of what could lie before them? It was one thing to know something was going to happen and quite another to be in the middle of it. Remembering his own basic training, Callum reflected that none of the training officers had ever openly spoken about the inevitable dangers they faced, not in any concrete way. His first active tour in East Timor had been a baptism by fire. He swore to himself he'd do his best to equip these recruits with the resilience they would need.

Billy just looked thoughtful at Callum's reply. He opened his mouth to say something else, but hesitated. Callum sighed, suddenly feeling a wave of exhaustion again. "Spit it out, Cassidy."

"I just wondered, sir...maybe it's a silly question...but is it worth it? Being in the army? Is it worth all the death?"

Callum stared at him. The boy's words were like a punch to the gut. It was a question he had no answer for. He looked around the room, his gaze settling briefly on every recruit before he spoke again. "That's something you'll have to answer for yourselves. I'll ask you in a few years." *If you're alive,* he thought before dismissing them.

THE REST of the day passed uneventfully. Parade Training was frustrating, and he tried to recall how it had been when he was a fresh recruit, green around the ears and knowing far less than he thought he did. Surely, though, he'd been able to march in a straight line.

After his duties finished, Callum went home to change into gym clothes. He'd pushed through his earlier tiredness with the help of a few too many coffees and now felt unpleasantly restless and jittery. If he tried to sleep while feeling like this, he was sure to have another nightmare. A good workout and hot shower would hopefully balance out both body and brain.

It had been a good first day, he reflected as he drove to the gym. Far from feeling like he had 'downgraded', he felt privileged to teach the latest cohort and pleased to discover he had an aptitude for something other than being a soldier. Even Parade Training had given him a sense of fulfilment when after two hours of drill, a basic formation—with everyone facing in the same direction—had been managed. Apart from Billy Cassidy's question, he'd remained in the moment all day, thoughts of his recent past behind him. Maybe this was what he needed.

He parked outside the gym in downtown Salford and got out of his car. A woman had left the building and was walking in his direction. Slim and toned, with honey blonde hair pulled back in a ponytail, something about her was familiar.

She frowned as she approached, as if she also sensed familiarity. When he saw her soft, blue eyes that were as clear as the sky above, and her cute, upturned nose, he felt a jolt of recognition. *Fleur Gibbons. Jeff's widow.*

He hesitated. Should he say hello, or would she find it intrusive? He needn't have worried. She gave him a shy smile. "Lieutenant...Westaway?"

"Lieutenant Colonel," he said with a smile, "or just Callum is fine. You're Fleur?"

"Yes." A shadow crossed her face. "I met you at Jeff's funeral. I remember your name—he always spoke highly of you when he was home on leave."

Callum wasn't sure whether he felt pleased or sad. Jeff had only been with his squadron a few months; they hadn't been close. Still, he'd liked the man and often thought in different circumstances they might have met for a drink. "Jeff was a good man."

Fleur bit her lip, looking away. "Yes," she said quietly. "He was."

There was a pause before Callum cleared his throat, feeling awkward at not knowing what to say in this situation. "So...how have you been?"

She met his gaze again. Her eyes were clear and he immediately felt she was someone to be trusted. Even at the funeral he'd noticed she had a certain poise about her. She gave another a small smile. "Good. It's taken a while to get to this point, but we did." She fingered a small silver cross around her neck as she spoke.

"It must have been hard," he said with compassion.

"It was. There were days when I felt the pain of loss would never get better. But it got easier with time. That's what they say, don't they? Time's a healer." She glanced down and tucked some hair behind her ear. "It feels like nonsense at the beginning, a thing people say because they don't know what else to say, but then you wake up one morning and realise it's a little easier to breathe."

She looked taken aback at how much she'd revealed and gave a breathy, embarrassed laugh. "Sorry, I don't know where all that came from."

Callum shook his head quickly. He'd been completely caught up in her words. "Not at all. I'm glad I saw you. I've often wondered how you were doing. Jeff talked about you and the children all the time—nearly drove the rest of us mad."

She let out a small laugh and he couldn't help noticing how her face lit up. "That's so nice to hear," she said before glancing at her wristwatch. "I wish we had longer to chat. It's so nice to talk to someone about Jeff after all these years. I don't see anyone from the army anymore, but I never was one to mingle with the wives." She frowned as if realising something. "Are you on leave?"

"Not quite. I've taken a break from active service. I'm based at Salford Barracks, overseeing the training of the new recruits." He felt embarrassed as he said it, so was gratified when she looked impressed.

"That's fantastic. I bet you're brilliant at it."

Callum was surprised to feel himself flush. "Well, the jury's out on that one; it was only my first day today. I usually work out first thing in the morning, but I guess it will have to be evenings from now on." He motioned towards the gym. "Are you here after work too?" He tried to remember if Jeff had spoken about Fleur having a career.

She grinned. "This is my work. I'm a gym instructor. Yoga, Pilates and CrossFit. Sometimes Aqua Aerobics, too."

"Wow. That's great. You must enjoy it."

"I love it," she said with a simple honesty he found appealing. As much as he'd been driven to get ahead in his army career, he didn't think he could ever have said those words with the obvious contentment she did.

"I'd just finished my training when Jeff died," she continued, "so working has been a real help. Gave me something outside to focus on. That and my faith." Her hand went subconsciously back to the cross around her neck.

Callum felt a pang of something that was close to envy. He'd never really understood faith, though he'd been taken to church services and attended Sunday School as a kid. That had been his father, keeping up appearances, rather than through any real commitment or belief. As far as Callum knew, his parents now only went to church at Christmas and Easter.

"I don't know much about that," he admitted, wishing suddenly he'd paid more attention in Sunday School. He realised he wanted to impress Fleur, but wasn't sure why. Something about her drew him, and it wasn't just the fact that she was extremely attractive. Was it a sense of guilt about Jeff that made him feel almost protective towards her? Although the explosion hadn't been his fault, he always retained a sense of responsibility for the men he'd lost. Losing men was something he'd never been able to get used to.

For an instant, wistfulness stole into her expression. "That's a pity." There was another silence before she smiled apologetically. "It was lovely seeing you, Lieutenant...Callum, but please excuse me. I've got to get back for the kids."

Callum didn't know if he imagined the expectant note in her words, but found himself asking, "Would you like to go for lunch sometime? You said it was nice to talk to someone from...back then. And, well, I don't really know anyone here off base."

It seemed an age before she answered, and Callum thought he'd misread her completely and was starting to wish the ground would swallow him up, when she nodded and gave that shy smile again. "That would be nice. Here," she swung her gym bag off her shoulder and reached into it, "here's my card."

"Thank you very much," he said, and then chastised himself for being so formal. He took the card and tucked it into the pocket of his shorts.

"Right, well. See you." She gave him one last smile before turning and heading down the road.

"Bye." He lifted his hand and watched her go, feeling bemused at their encounter. Such a coincidence that he'd bumped into her the day after dreaming about Jeff.

That was why he felt drawn to her. And it'd be nice to have at least an acquaintance here who wasn't from the base. Yes, that was it.

The fact that she was extremely attractive and made him feel like a nervous schoolboy had nothing to do with it at all.

CHAPTER 2

"*M*um! You're not listening," ten-year-old Lucy complained from the back of the car.

"Sorry sweetheart," Fleur said guiltily. "Say that again."

She tried to pay attention as her daughter painstakingly went back over the details of her best friend Marsha's current argument with their classmate Jessie, which had all started when Jessie started copying Marsha's hair ribbon. Fleur tried to remind herself that for a ten-year-old girl, these topics were of the utmost importance, but this morning she was more distracted on the school run than usual.

Her thoughts kept turning to Callum Westaway and their chance encounter. Bumping into him had been a pleasant surprise, but now she wasn't sure how she felt about it. Had he thought her forward for giving him her card? Or worse, that she was flirting? *That would be so embarrassing.*

It would be nice to see him again, though, if only to talk about Jeff now that the grief wasn't so raw. The first year after his death, she'd felt as though she were moving through thick fog, going through the motions in order to keep some kind of consistency for the children. It had been the second year that the grief had hit her, the last remnants of the shock and denial giving way to deep sadness and anger.

God and her children had been her saving grace. Now, after more than three years of widowhood, the pain was bittersweet, an enduring sorrow mixed with memories that still sometimes made her cry, but more often than not, brought a smile to her face. She still missed Jeff, but with a sense of nostalgia rather than the acute pain of before.

Despite supportive friends and her parents, who'd been a refuge for them these past few years, Fleur often felt lonely, especially in the evenings. Her best friend Amy was happily married, and recently Fleur had started to feel very much like 'the single friend'. Still, she was nowhere near ready for a relationship. Something she repeatedly told Amy to no avail, as her friend resolutely attempted to set her up with every eligible bachelor in the small town of Salford, particularly if they came to their church. Fleur smiled to herself as she thought of Amy. She was looking forward to seeing her this afternoon for Bible group.

"Girls are stupid," eight-year-old Will announced, apparently musing on his sister's problems.

"Mum! Will's being sexist," Lucy complained. "Don't call people stupid, Will."

"Well, they are," Will muttered. In the rear-view mirror, Fleur saw him settle into his seat sulkily before sticking his tongue out at Lucy.

"Mum!" Lucy wailed again. Fleur sighed, grateful when she

pulled into the lay-by near the school playground. She loved her children with a ferocity that could still take her breath away, but she doubted if the morning school run was any parent's favourite time of day.

As she saw them into their respective classrooms, she watched them go with pride. Jeff's passing had been devastating for the children, too, but they were resilient little souls and had made great progress in the last year. It was funny, though, she worried about Will more now, even though he'd only been five when his dad died and he hadn't really understood what had happened.

His bewildered questions of 'When is Daddy coming back?' had been heart-breaking, but easier to deal with than Lucy's bedwetting and refusal to speak for weeks after they received the news. Now, though, Lucy seemed to have integrated the loss better than Will, who had refused to go to a birthday party last week because 'I'm the only one without a Dad.' Fleur had cried herself to sleep that night, something that hadn't happened for months. In the end, her father had persuaded Will to go and had dropped him off and picked him up. She thanked God for her father, who had stepped in as a male role model for his grandchildren.

Fleur got back into her car and drove to work. She only had two classes this morning, and this afternoon was her Women's Bible study group. As she walked into Salford Leisure Centre, thoughts of bumping into Callum the day before once again crossed her mind. It seemed he was a regular here. Once more, concern that she'd been too forward by pressing her card onto him washed over her. What if he never called and then she bumped into him again? That would be awkward.

But then, he'd been the one who suggested meeting up. She recalled his words about not knowing anyone other than fellow army mates. It must be a lonely life, she reflected, without anybody to come home to.

She put thoughts of Callum to one side and prepared for class. CrossFit was first, which she loved, especially helping people to improve each week and push past their self-imposed barriers. Then a gentle yoga session, a nice contrast to the mirrors and pumping music in the CrossFit class.

After the two sessions, she showered and changed from her gym clothes to jeans and a T-shirt and made her way to Amy's. It was her friend's turn to host their group this week.

"Hey, beautiful." Amy enveloped her in a floral scented hug. Fleur grinned and squeezed her back. They'd been best friends since high school, and Fleur couldn't imagine what she'd do without her. Blonde, bubbly and curvaceous, Amy cultivated a ditzy demeanour that belied a sharp wit and eye that noticed everything. Indeed, as they stepped into the kitchen to make up the tea tray for the rest of the group, she cocked her head to one side and regarded Fleur, pursing her lips. "Something's happened," she said. "You seem...jittery. But not in a bad way."

Fleur shrugged. "I have no idea what you're talking about. It's been a pretty standard morning." Callum Westaway appeared in her mind's eye. "Well...I bumped into Jeff's old officer last night, but that's not particularly significant."

"That Westwood guy you spoke to at the funeral?"

"It's Westaway. But yes, he's relocated to Salford and has started teaching at the base." Fleur couldn't explain why she felt her cheeks flame under Amy's piercing gaze.

Her friend put her hands on her hips. "That's it!" she said

with a touch of triumph. "You swapped numbers, didn't you? Please tell me you did. You wouldn't have noticed at Jeff's funeral, of course, but I did. The guy is seriously handsome."

Fleur shook her head, though she felt a smile tugging the corner of her lips. "It wasn't like that at all. He mentioned possibly meeting up because he doesn't know many people here. I gave him my card. Honestly Amy, you see romance everywhere. Are you sure things are okay with Angus?"

"Uh-uh," Amy wagged her finger. "You're not doing that. Things are great with me and Angus. Stop deflecting. Seriously, Fleur, you didn't notice how good looking he is?"

Fleur threw up her hands in defeat. "Okay, yes, of course I did. But it really wasn't about that at all. I very much doubt he'll even call."

Amy raised her brows. "You didn't get his number? Fleur, honestly, what am I going to do with you?"

"Right now, you can help me with this tea tray." Fleur turned around and busied herself with the cups, sensing rather than seeing Amy grinning at her back.

THANKFULLY, hosting Bible group distracted Amy from Fleur's lack of a romantic life. Fleur soon found herself forgetting all about her outside cares as the women prayed together and then turned to their current study scripture.

They were studying Ephesians, which she was glad about as it was her favourite book of scripture. Its theme of the abundance of God's grace had been a great comfort to her in the last few years, as had the emphasis on finding a new identity in the Lord. It reminded her that she wasn't just her various roles:

Jeff's widow, Will and Lucy's mother, a gym instructor, even 'the single friend'. She was a child of God and beloved of Christ, an identity that went right to her core. All else flowed from that. With that, she knew, she could get through anything.

Today however, they were looking at Ephesians chapter five, verses twenty-two and twenty-three. It was the section on a loving marriage, and Fleur couldn't help feel a pang of grief as the other women discussed the passage in light of either their current marriage or hopes for one. She was the only widow there. For once, she didn't have much to contribute to the discussion and was glad when they moved on to the next section on families and workplaces. Next week was spiritual warfare. At the mention of conflict, she thought of both Jeff and Callum, and wondered not for the first time at how actual warfare must affect one's soul.

After the group finished and the other women had left, Fleur quickly tidied the cups away and pulled her bag over her shoulder. It was nearly time to pick up Lucy and Will, which meant there wasn't an opportunity for Amy to continue quizzing her about Callum.

"Angus is going fishing this evening," Amy said as they hugged goodbye. "I could come round if you're free?"

Fleur smiled. Amy knew that apart from church and visiting her parents, she was almost always free in the evenings. "Of course. Come at seven and help me put the kids to bed if you like. I know you love reading Lucy a story, and she loves the way you act out all the parts."

Amy grinned. "I know, I've missed my calling. I should have been an actress." Amy worked as HR Manager at a local renewable energy company, a job she liked, but didn't overly love.

"No needling me about Callum Westaway," Fleur warned.

Amy smiled innocently. "Would I?" She winked at Fleur as she left, causing Fleur to shake her head in amused exasperation.

LATER, Fleur poured two apple juices and leaned against the kitchen counter. Listening to Amy's animated voice drifting down the stairs as she read Lucy a story, and Lucy's snorts of laughter, she smiled to herself, thinking not for the first time how blessed she was to have Amy as her friend. She'd been her confidante since high school, and they'd been there for each other through pretty much everything. Although being widowed had been the hardest thing Fleur had ever had to face, it had made her realise how fortunate she was to have the support of people like Amy and her parents.

She thought again of Callum Westaway and how lonely he'd seemed. Or at least, that was the impression she'd gained. They'd only spoken for a few minutes, she reminded herself, and here she was psychoanalysing the poor guy. Jeff had always teased her about being 'a rescuer' and wanting to help everybody, but she couldn't help the way she was. From rescuing fallen baby birds to mentoring younger, less privileged children at school, she'd always had an uncanny ability to respond to the brokenness in people.

She looked up as Amy came down the stairs. "Is she asleep? She was laughing her head off a moment ago."

Amy nodded. "Yep. Out like a light. I told you, I've got the touch."

"You certainly have." Fleur smiled, and then noticed a shadow cross Amy's face. Amy and Angus had been trying for over a year now to start a family, so far with no luck. Amy had confided in her last week that they were going for tests at the fertility clinic.

Before Fleur could respond, the shadow was gone as soon as it had appeared, to be replaced by Amy's usual bright smile. "Did Will go down okay?"

"Yes, he was exhausted from football." Fleur passed Amy her drink, which she accepted with a grateful nod, before kicking off her pumps and sitting on the couch. Fleur sat next to her, tucking her legs underneath her. The two sipped their drinks in silence for a moment before Amy looked at Fleur with a glint in her eye. "So...any word from the dashing lieutenant yet?"

"Amy! You promised. And it's Lieutenant Colonel."

"I promised not to needle you. I'm not needling. It was a perfectly innocent question." Amy did her best impression of an innocent look.

"You look like a rabbit caught in the headlights." Fleur giggled and shook her head. "But honestly, there's nothing to talk about. He mentioned not having any friends in town, so I passed him my card. It'd be nice to go for lunch, perhaps. Anyway, he probably won't even call." Realising she was talking too fast, she took a large mouthful of juice and wondered what she was getting so flustered about.

"Will you be disappointed?"

"If he doesn't call?" Fleur hesitated, unsure what the honest answer to Amy's question was. If he didn't call, then it didn't matter, surely? It probably meant he'd found other ways to get settled into Salford, which was a good thing. "I don't think so. I don't know if it's even a good idea to befriend someone who worked with Jeff. As much as it's nice to speak to someone who knew that side of him..." Her words trailed off as sadness washed over her.

Amy laid a hand over hers. "You don't need to talk about it if you don't want to," she said in a soft voice.

Fleur shrugged. "Sometimes I want to hold on to his memory, you know, keep it alive. Especially for the children. But other times I feel like we need to move on, but then I feel guilty. Like I'm saying it's okay to forget about him. Even his face is fuzzy sometimes." She looked down, blinking back tears, shocked at the sudden flood of emotion running through her.

Amy squeezed her hand. "It's okay, Fleur. Jeff wouldn't want you to mourn forever. It doesn't mean you, or the kids, are ever going to forget him."

Fleur nodded. She knew that, logically, but rarely did emotions listen to reason.

"Blessed are those who mourn, for they will be comforted," Amy said, quoting from the book of Matthew.

Fleur wiped her eyes. "That's one of my favourite passages." And the words were so true, she reminded herself. God had been her comfort and her rock in the dark days after Jeff's death. "Thank you," she said to Amy with a smile.

The shrill ring of the telephone startled them both.

"It'll be Mum." Fleur quickly crossed the floor and picked up the receiver. "Hey Mum. You've just missed the kids, they're already in bed. Amy read Lucy a story; I think she laughed herself to sleep."

There was a pause on the other end, and then a man's voice, sounding both hesitant and amused. "Fleur? I have no idea who Amy and Lucy are, but they sound delightful. It's Callum Westaway."

Fleur felt her cheeks flame.

Amy straightened and cocked a brow. "Is it him?" she whispered loudly.

Fleur waved a hand at her to be quiet, feeling her cheeks burn even more. "Callum, hi!" She winced as her voice came out in a high pitch. "I'm sorry, I wasn't expecting you."

There was another pause. "I hope it's okay to call. You gave me your card...I was going to suggest lunch this week, but please, don't worry if you're busy." He sounded embarrassed now.

Fleur took a deep breath. "No, its fine," she reassured him in a more normal tone of voice. "I'd love to. How about Thursday? I've got classes in the morning, so I could meet you outside the gym about half-past twelve? There's a nice little café over the road." She covered the mouthpiece, hoping Callum didn't hear Amy's sudden squeal of excitement.

"That would be great." He sounded relieved.

Fleur paused before saying, "Well, I'll see you there," more brusquely than she intended, while trying to ignore Amy and her excited face.

"Yes, I'll look forward to it. See you then," Callum replied, more formally now.

There was another awkward pause before Fleur replaced the handset, momentarily placing her head in her hands before looking up to glare at Amy. "Honestly! You're acting like a schoolgirl," she admonished her friend.

"So, what's happening? You're meeting him? What are you going to wear? Please don't tell me you're just going to stay in your sweaty gym clothes."

"Amy!" Fleur threw a cushion at her before bursting into giggles. She collapsed onto the couch next to her friend, her mind whirling. It was just lunch, she told herself firmly. No big deal. She was just flustered because of Amy being silly and teasing her.

No, her heart *definitely* hadn't fluttered when she'd heard the sound of his voice, but the pang of guilt at her self-dishonesty confirmed otherwise.

CHAPTER 3

*C*allum nodded at the recruits as he dismissed them and glanced at the clock. Twelve hundred hours. He was meeting Fleur in thirty minutes. Nervousness bubbled in the bottom of his gut. What was wrong with him? It was just a friendly lunch, and if he were honest with himself, he was hoping that speaking to Jeff's wife and seeing she was doing well might help with the nightmares.

Mercifully, the last few nights had been dream-free, and he felt more rested than he had in weeks. He was amazed at how much he was enjoying his first week in his new post. While Military History and Parade Training were hardly fascinating subjects, he found himself becoming quickly invested in his recruits, wanting to encourage their journeys and see them succeed. It was a nice feeling.

So far Billy Cassidy, the young man Jarrop had warned him about, was exceeding expectations. He seemed eager to prove himself and clearly saw Callum as a role model. Callum wasn't sure how he felt about that. It was flattering, but he'd felt a similar responsibility to his men in the field.

And I couldn't always protect them. He sighed, trying to put his morbid thoughts to one side. He didn't want to take that attitude into lunch with Fleur; she'd been through enough.

He glanced at the clock again as he tidied his papers away. He'd thrown slacks and a shirt into his bag, but realised he'd forgotten spare shoes. He also realistically didn't have time to change. He'd have to meet Fleur in his uniform. He hoped it wouldn't revive bad memories for her.

FLEUR STOOD OUTSIDE THE GYM, twisting her hands together. There was really no need to feel so nervous. She'd ignored Amy's texts that morning wishing her all the best and demanding to know what she was wearing. Even so, she'd heeded her friend's advice and packed a change of clothes. She was wearing a simple jersey dress with a denim jacket and pumps, and at the last minute had added a pretty floral scarf she'd owned for months but never worn. Freshly washed, her hair curled around her shoulders. She'd felt slightly guilty as she'd sprayed herself with perfume and added a slick of lip gloss. It had been a while since she'd bothered with either.

She looked up. A man in army uniform was walking towards her, and her thoughts immediately went to Jeff, but this wasn't Jeff. The man was taller, broader and as much as she hated to admit it, more handsome. She swallowed hard as she recognised Callum. Her neck felt hot under her scarf.

"Hey," she said lightly, trying not to let her admiration show as he stopped beside her.

He smiled, looking down at himself uncertainly. "Sorry for the uniform. I didn't have time to change. For an army guy, I could definitely be more organised."

Fleur smiled. "You look great. Shall we head across the road?" She pointed up the road a little way to the café she'd mentioned to him on the phone.

"Sure. I'm more than ready to eat."

"So am I," she said with a small laugh.

They crossed the street together, and she smiled when he stepped in front to hold the door open for her. They chose a table beside the window, looking out on the park.

"I don't know Salford very well, although I've already been here a few weeks," he said.

"Do you live at the barracks?"

"No. I live in one of those new army townhouses."

Fleur winced. She and Jeff had been waiting for one of the army townhouses, but then, after he died, she'd used some of his insurance payout to put a mortgage down on her current property, a three-bedroom house on the other side of town, away from all the army housing. She hadn't wanted to stay in army property after he'd gone. Indeed, until she bumped into Callum, she'd had as little as possible to do with the military. "Do you think you'll stay there?"

"I expect so. I've got no intention of returning to active duty, though technically I could be called up anytime if they need me."

Fleur sensed the hidden emotion in his words. "And you wouldn't want that?"

He sighed and toyed with his glass of water. "I feel like I shouldn't say it, but honestly, no, I'm hoping that never happens. I've had a great career in the field, but I remember my commanding officer telling me years ago it's got a shelf life. I'd lost my passion towards the end."

He looked away, and Fleur sensed he felt embarrassed at his openness. She waved at the waitress, breaking the tension. Callum ordered a hamburger with chips, and looked amazed when Fleur ordered the same, but with an extra patty.

She laughed. "I've just done two hours of CrossFit. I'm absolutely starving."

He laughed with her. "I suppose it's a bit like PT drills. I used to eat like a Trojan afterwards."

"How are you finding your new position?" she asked after the waitress left.

"I'm really enjoying it." He answered with a genuine grin that caused his eyes to crinkle at the corners. Fleur had to agree with Amy; he really was a very handsome man. Tanned and toned in a purely natural way, with toffee brown hair that was just starting to sprinkle with grey, hazel eyes and soft, full lips that were normally a feminine feature but somehow served to make him look more masculine. Realising she was staring, she turned her focus to her hands which were wrapped around her glass of water.

Seemingly unaware of her appraisal, he continued. "I was worried I'd find it a bit dull, but I'm actually enjoying working with the recruits. It's more fulfilling than I thought it would be."

"Maybe that could be a new career option for you," she suggested. "Teaching."

His smile faded. "Maybe. The thing is, I've only ever known the army. I wouldn't have a clue about how to start working on Civvy Street."

Fleur nodded and stared out the window into the distance. "Jeff used to say the same." She released a breath and returned her gaze to her glass. "It used to worry me; I didn't want to be an army wife forever. I never said that to him, though, because I felt too guilty." She lifted her gaze. "But deep down I used to hope that he'd come home one day and announce he was leaving."

Callum frowned and looked a little uncomfortable. "I'm sorry he never had that chance," he said quietly.

His reaction surprised her. "You don't blame yourself, do you? I was told what happened; you were ambushed."

"Logically, no, but there's a part of me that feels responsible for every one of the men I lost. That I should have been able to protect them. It's silly, of course; we all knew the risks. But knowing something and feeling it are two different things."

Her heart went out to him as she heard the sadness in his voice. She started to respond empathetically when a thought struck her; was this why he wanted to meet her, to alleviate his own misplaced sense of guilt?

She opened her mouth to say something, but as if knowing her thoughts, he answered them when he said, "It was so good to see you and know you're doing okay. I felt a little awkward asking you for lunch given the circumstances. I don't want you to think it was just because of Jeff. I mean, not entirely. It was just good to see a semi-familiar face outside the barracks."

Relief washed over her. Although, if she were honest, her whole reason for giving him her card in the first place was because of Jeff, wasn't it? They wouldn't have spoken to each other otherwise. Perhaps it wasn't a bad thing that they had that shared experience. Would Jeff approve of their meeting up like this? She thought he would. Jeff had a big heart.

It was funny though, now that they were here, she didn't want to speak about Jeff. She was more interested in knowing about Callum. "Do you think you'll feel responsible for the recruits too?" she asked.

He looked thoughtful, then sighed and nodded. "Yes. It hasn't escaped me that that's the fate I'm preparing some of them for. They're so naïve. I keep looking at them and thinking, was I like that?" He gave a half laugh and shook his head.

The waitress arrived with their food, and the conversation stopped for a while as they ate, other than the occasional comment about how tasty it was. Callum laughed as Fleur polished off her slightly larger meal before he finished his.

"I told you I've got an appetite!"

"It's good to see. Not that I have much experience with women these days, but I remember my wife and her friends seemed to be constantly on diets."

Fleur's forehead crinkled. "I didn't know you were married."

"It was a long time ago. Danielle didn't want to be an army wife either. She's remarried now, with children. I'm glad she's happy."

"And you?" Fleur asked softly. "Are you happy?"

Callum's gaze lifted to meet hers, and for just a moment, she saw overwhelming sadness in his eyes.

"I can't complain," he said brusquely, the sadness disappearing as if it had never been there. He finished his food, clearly not wanting to continue that line of conversation.

"I'm sorry. It was a personal question." She winced at her forthrightness.

Callum wiped his mouth with his napkin and shook his head. "Not at all," he said in his usual tone. "I asked after you, too. I suppose it's just not a question I'm used to being asked. Colonel Jarrop isn't in the habit of asking after my happiness in the mornings in between barking orders."

Fleur grinned at the picture he painted of his superior. "Yes, I suppose it wouldn't be the thing to do. They do look after soldiers emotionally, though? I know Jeff used to get a lot out of visiting the chaplain."

Callum shifted in his seat. "Not really. I mean, yes, there are the chaplains, but if you're not religious, visiting them isn't normal. Counselling is offered after a particularly gruelling tour, but it's not commonplace for anyone to take it up. There's a real culture of dealing with things by yourself. Getting over it. We're soldiers, and it's what we signed up for."

Fleur shook her head. "What about those who are really struggling?"

Calum shrugged again and rubbed his neck. Fleur wanted to kick herself. Why couldn't she just chat about the weather, or something else mundane? She wished Amy were here. Amy was great at small talk.

She looked out the window again, and then had an idea. "Do you have to hurry back? There's a lovely path by the river just behind the museum over there, if you fancy a walk."

His lips twitched, but then he smiled his crinkly-eyed smile again. "That sounds great."

They finished their drinks and split the bill at Fleur's insistence and headed off towards the river. Passing a trio of women coming towards them with shopping bags, Fleur couldn't help but notice how they all looked Callum up and down with admiration dripping from their eyes. He didn't seem to notice.

"I think your uniform is attracting attention." She chuckled but wondered why she felt a little annoyed as the women walked off giggling.

"It usually does," Callum said without a touch of arrogance. "I've never really understood it myself."

She could understand exactly why it did.

AS THEY STROLLED along the riverside, Callum couldn't help glancing sideways at Fleur. She was so pretty, in a natural and non-self-obsessed way, seemingly unaware of how gorgeous she looked in her simple outfit that brought out the blue of her eyes. He admonished himself, reminding himself she was Jeff's wife—widow—and he hadn't asked her for lunch with the intention of dating her. That would be grossly inappropriate.

But would it? After three years? Callum ignored his thoughts and instead pointed to a brightly coloured houseboat travelling slowly down the river. "That looks fun."

Fleur nodded. "Yes, my mum and dad keep talking about buying a houseboat when they retire. They're so slow though —you wouldn't get anywhere fast. I suppose that's the point."

"Are your parents local?" Callum thought, with a pang of guilt, that he wouldn't want to live much nearer to his parents.

He loved them, but he preferred to love his father, in particular, from a distance.

"Yes, they live on the other side of Salford. They've been a great help with the kids. Them and my friends from church."

"You mentioned church before." Callum wasn't sure what to make of her obvious faith. In all his years in the army, he'd never spoken to the chaplains, and church services had become an occasional formality.

"Yes, my faith is really important to me. I take it you don't share it?"

There was no judgment in her voice, just genuine curiosity, but even so, Callum felt the need to defend himself. "Well, I'm Anglican. But it's not something I've ever really practiced as such. To be honest, I've never given it much thought."

Fleur angled her head. "I suppose that's true for a lot of people. Doing what you guys do though, staring death in the face all day, I wonder how you get through those traumas without a belief in God. Doesn't it all seem pointless sometimes?"

Her words stunned him, and he answered honestly before he could stop himself. "Yes. Sometimes it does. I suppose that's why I wanted to leave. The death, the killing, the endless months away from any real civilisation. I started to ask myself that very question. What's the point? But then I think, what would happen if we had no defence force? There's real evil out there. And then I suppose the question is, if there's a God that loves and cares about us, why does He allow all this carnage?" He stopped, shocked at his own outburst. "I'm sorry, I didn't mean to question what you believe..."

"Its fine," she cut him off. "It's human to ask questions like that. My faith in God deepened after wrestling with very similar questions after Jeff died. There were so many nights when my only prayer was '*why?*'"

"Then how do you reconcile it?" Callum realised he was genuinely interested in the answer.

"God didn't create war; men did. Jesus' whole message is one of peace and reconciliation. Justice too, of course, but also grace and mercy. It's humans who choose to act against that in their greed and hatred."

Callum blew out a heavy breath. "I think you're right. I suppose it's easier to blame something outside of ourselves, isn't it?"

"Of course." Smiling, Fleur reached for the cross around her neck. "But I don't think of God as something 'outside.' I know it's hard to understand, but He lives in me. Although all of this beauty was also created by Him." She swept her arm to indicate the scenery around them. The shady trees, the slow flowing river, the garden beds filled with flowering natives. "We focus too much on what's wrong, but often don't notice the beauty around us." Her face was radiant as she spoke about her beliefs.

He nodded. "You're right. I think I've become so accustomed to witnessing atrocities, I often don't see the good in anything." He hadn't addressed her earlier statement, but it intrigued him. *How could God live in her?* Although it sounded strange, something about it tugged at him. "I wish I had your faith," he said.

She smiled. "You can."

Their gazes met for a moment before he looked away. For some reason, this woman he barely knew seemed able to penetrate through all of his defences, reaching a vulnerable place he rarely showed anyone. If ever.

AS THEY STROLLED BACK, Fleur turned the conversation to lighter subjects, chatting about the kids and Amy and her plans for a holiday next year. Callum told her about one of his recruits, a young man called Billy who appeared to have signed up in a last-ditch attempt to save himself from a life of crime and was doing really well. Fleur could hear in his voice how Callum was cheering for the young man and noticed again how his face lit up when he spoke about guiding the recruits. Did he realise that he may have found his new calling?

A moment of awkwardness occurred as they stood beside her car before Callum rather formally shook her hand. "Thank you for today, it was really nice. I'd better get back to barracks, but, see you soon?"

"Yes, of course. I had a lovely time. Thank you." As he walked away, she felt a tinge of disappointment. They hadn't arranged when they'd see each other again. Perhaps he wouldn't want to, now that he knew she was doing okay and could lay whatever guilt he was feeling to rest. But he said their getting together today wasn't just about Jeff.

Honestly, you're acting like a schoolgirl, she told herself crossly as she got into the car. It had been lunch with an acquaintance, nothing more. Yet, she couldn't help but think about the sadness she'd seen in his eyes when he spoke about his time in the field, and the glimpse of longing she'd sensed in him when she spoke about her faith.

He's longing for You, Lord, he just doesn't realise it.

Perhaps that was the reason they'd bumped into each other. Perhaps she was meant to lead him to the Lord. The moment the thought hit her, she felt an upwelling sense of calm and she bowed her head and prayed.

Lord God, I pray that Callum finds his way to You. That he realises that You're his strength and refuge, and the One who can truly heal his wounds. If I'm to be any part of his journey, may I be so with a glad and willing heart. Please guide and lead me. In Jesus' precious name. Amen.

Feeling renewed, she drove off, giving one last look in her rear-view mirror as Callum disappeared from sight.

CHAPTER 4

*O*ver the next few days, Fleur found it difficult to stop thinking about Callum. She kept remembering the haunted look in his eyes, and his eager but conflicted questions about God. She continued to pray for him in her usual morning and evening prayer times, and at other odd occasions throughout the day.

When the weekend passed and the next week was nearly halfway through, she realised she hadn't heard from him. She tried to ignore her disappointment, but by the time Tuesday afternoon came around and she was sitting on Amy's patio while Will and Lucy played in the backyard, she found herself talking about him as the sun dropped lower in the sky and the cockatoos gathered nosily in the large blue-gum outside Amy's fence line.

"He seemed so conflicted when we were talking. I'd like to invite him to church, but I don't know if that would be too forward."

"Just do it. But you can't take responsibility for him, Fleur. Let God do His work in him."

"Yes, but..." Her voice trailed off. She didn't know why she felt so invested in this man she barely knew, but she instinctively felt that this was more than her usual tendency to want to help anyone who was suffering. She felt a connection to Callum she couldn't quite name. "Maybe it's Jeff. Maybe by helping Callum I feel I'm doing something for Jeff. I don't know." She shrugged and stared at the mug of tea in her hands.

"I don't think this is about Jeff. Not really," Amy said. "And I know I said I'd stop teasing you about it, so I will, but let's be real here, Fleur. Is it really beyond the realm of possibility that you two may actually *like* each other? More than friends, I mean?"

"I don't think I'm ready for more than friends," Fleur said honestly. "Plus, he's not a believer."

"Yet. And besides, you can't be on your own forever. You're only thirty-four."

"I know, but... I've gotten so used to thinking of myself as a widow, it's hard to contemplate anything else. With Callum or anyone."

"What about the kids?" Amy motioned towards Will and Lucy, who for once had put aside their sibling differences to play a convoluted game of pirates and spacemen.

"What about them?"

"I'm not saying they need a father figure. You're a brilliant parent, but it wouldn't hurt them to have a good male role model in their lives."

"They have my Dad. And Angus."

"Both admirable men, if I do say so." Amy grinned. "But even so…"

Fleur shook her head. "I couldn't risk hurting them." She watched Will and Lucy playing, while a pang of raw grief at the loss they'd both endured so young gripped her heart.

"I know. Just trust God, Fleur. You never know what He has in store for you."

"You're right. I haven't heard from Callum, anyway."

"Have you contacted him?"

Fleur shook her head. "No! How forward would that be?"

Amy raised a perfectly arched eyebrow. "Not at all, if you're just friends. I've got an idea. You know I said we were having a barbecue this weekend?"

Fleur shook her head as she realised where Amy was going with this. "No. No way. That would look too much like a date, and I don't want to go there."

"It's a family event, not the two of you and the two of us. Lots of people from church will be here. Think about it. What a perfect opportunity for him to meet other people who could help bring him to the Lord."

Fleur nodded slowly. Amy was right. Callum had said he didn't know anyone, and she definitely felt called to guide him to Christ. Inviting him to a social function was a great idea, and with the kids and Amy and Angus and everyone else around, it wouldn't look like a date at all. It could be good for him. "Okay. I'll think about it."

Amy tutted. "Don't think, do. The barbecue is Friday evening and you need to give him a few days' notice. You have his number, don't you?"

Fleur nodded. She'd made a note of it when he called her.

"Then, what are you waiting for?"

～

CALLUM DRUMMED his fingers on the table, staring at his phone. He hadn't heard from Fleur and had spent every evening since their lunch wondering whether or not he should call her.

He wanted to see her again. He'd been amazed at how easy it had been to talk with her, and the quiet understanding she'd offered when he shared with her things he'd never shared with anyone before. He couldn't remember ever being so at ease talking about his feelings, even as a child. Although he'd been able to go to his mother with anything, he'd also absorbed the idea from his father that men should be stoic, and the older he got, the more he tried to be like him, and the less he'd confided in his mother.

It wasn't that his father hadn't been good to him. He was a great man, but he'd always had certain expectations that Callum had constantly tried to live up to. Never had he heard his father talk negatively about his experiences in the army or show any signs of having been emotionally affected. Somehow, ever since the nightmares had started and he'd battled the feelings they provoked in him, Callum hadn't been able to shake the sense that he was letting his father down.

With Fleur, though, it had felt alright, as though she understood, and he'd sensed no judgment from her. Only empathy.

Not only that, he enjoyed her company. When was the last time he'd had a female friend? Or any friend except his fellow soldiers, for that matter? And as he'd moved up the ranks, there'd been even more of a barrier between him and his men.

So, he should call her. But what if she didn't want him to? He was sure she had plenty of friends. She probably didn't need him hanging around. She'd probably only agreed to lunch in the first place to be kind.

Then there was the fact that he was attracted to her. He'd tried to avoid even thinking about that, but now that he was on his own with no distractions, he couldn't lie to himself—Fleur Gibbons was downright gorgeous. He hadn't noticed a woman that way in...he didn't even know how long. There'd been a few girlfriends since Danielle, but never anyone serious. He hadn't wanted to get hurt again, and so he'd put his career above all else. It had been easier that way. Easier than trying to manage the demands of marriage on top of the demands of the army. Military wives—and husbands too, these days—took a big back seat to the Forces. They had to, or the job wouldn't get done.

Now, though, Callum found himself wondering what it had all been for. All these years of devoted service, and for what? A divorce, an empty three-bedroom townhouse and a teaching job in a town with less than twenty thousand inhabitants. Some medals, yes, commendations of bravery, the pride of his parents...but none of those made him any less lonely.

Or stopped the nightmares.

With a sigh, he pushed the phone away. He wasn't going to phone Fleur, tonight or any night. She was an army widow. She'd been through enough and had come out the other side. The last thing she needed was him with all his baggage.

Feeling morose, he stood and trudged to the fridge, intending to crack open a beer, when his phone rang. He turned around, feeling a jolt in his stomach when he saw the name flashing on the screen.

Fleur.

His low mood momentarily forgotten and his chest fluttering, he answered the phone. "Hello Fleur. It's good to hear from you." He hoped he didn't sound too eager.

"Hey," she said warmly, then hesitated. "How are you?"

"Great, thanks. I was actually thinking of calling you when you rang," he said lightly, as if it had been a passing thought rather than a source of torment for the past hour.

"Oh really?" Callum was sure she sounded pleased.

"Yes, I really enjoyed lunch. I hope I didn't go on too much," he said.

"Not at all. It was great getting to know you a little. I was thinking," her voice sped up, her words coming out in a rush, "if you're free this Friday, my friend Amy is having a barbecue."

"Oh?" Was she inviting him?

"Yes, er....I know you mentioned about not knowing any people in the area, and as there'll be quite a few there, I thought it might be a nice way to help you settle in. I'm going with the kids, so it's an informal thing."

Callum felt a twinge of disappointment. For a moment he'd thought she was asking him on a kind of date. He didn't want to examine the flutter of excitement that possibility had given him. Still, he thought, it was lovely of her to think of him. "That sounds nice, but won't your friend think it's a bit of an imposition?"

Fleur laughed, and the sound warmed him. "Oh no, the more the merrier as far as Amy's concerned. It was actually her idea."

A smile tugged at Callum's lips. Fleur had mentioned him to her friend? "That sounds great. I don't have any other plans," he said honestly.

"So, you'll come?"

"Yes." He grinned. "I'll come." Maybe it wasn't a date, but an afternoon spent making friends with people who weren't in the army sounded great.

"I'm so glad." Relief sounded in Fleur's voice. "Would you like to meet me there, or come with me? I mean, because you don't know anyone," she said hurriedly. She obviously didn't want him to get the wrong idea, he realised, and though he felt a plunge of disappointment, there was a feeling of relief too. He couldn't deal with any more complicated feelings right now, could he? "It'd be great to go together. Just let me know the time and your address."

Fleur gave him her address and he reached in the drawer for pen and paper and wrote it down. There was an awkward silence until they both asked at the same time, "So, how was your day?"

Fleur laughed. "Snap!"

Callum chuckled. He hadn't heard that expression since school. "You go first."

"It was great. I had three classes today but I've mostly got private clients for the rest of the week. And yours?"

"Good," Callum answered. He'd been proud of the recruits today.

"So, are you feeling better about things?" she asked, a more serious tone in her voice.

Callum sighed, not really knowing what to say. He was still enjoying his new position, but the more he got to know the

43

young men and women he was training, the more he felt like the last thing he wanted to do was send them off to war. Boys like Cassidy, eager to prove themselves as 'tough' would volunteer straight away for the frontline. The thought of Billy ending up like Jeff and so many others he'd known made him shudder.

"Sorry," Fleur said quickly when he didn't answer. "That was nosey of me."

"Not at all," Callum hastened to reassure her. "I suppose I just don't know what the answer to your question is." Once again, he found himself easily confiding in her as he explained his feelings.

"It sounds really difficult," she said softly. "I know this might sound a bit drastic, but...have you wondered if the army is the right place for you right now?"

Callum sucked in air. It was the very question he kept asking himself. He released his breath slowly and replied, "I wouldn't know what else to do."

"I'm sure you have loads of skills that would transfer onto Civvy Street."

He shrugged. "Maybe. I think I've taken it for granted for so many years that I'd be in the army until it's time to get my pension. It feels alien to even consider otherwise. I'm from a military family," he explained, "and my father would be disappointed in me if he knew I was questioning things like this."

"Surely your father just wants the best for you?"

Callum sighed again. He didn't doubt it, but he was pretty sure his idea of 'best' and his father's weren't going to match up any time soon. "He does. But he also has a lot of expectations I don't think I'll ever live up to." A wave of sadness swept over him.

Fleur was quiet before she spoke again, in a voice filled with conviction. "I don't know your earthly father, Callum, but I do know something. Your Heavenly Father only wants the best for you, with no conditions attached. He loves you unconditionally, and there's not a thing you can do or a medal you can be awarded that can earn it."

Although he wasn't sure that he fully understood her words, they hit him like a sucker punch to the gut. Emotion welled up inside, and he realised he was gripping the phone tightly. "You really believe that, don't you?"

"No." Conviction throbbed in her voice. "I *know* it."

Again, he envied the simplicity of her devotion. How would it feel, to move through the world knowing you were loved like that? "Maybe I'll come to church one day," he said, surprising himself.

"That would be amazing!" He knew he wasn't imagining the happiness in her words.

They chatted a little longer, making small talk, until Fleur heard her son Will wake up and had to go. Callum said goodbye and went upstairs, amazed at how much lighter he felt from just speaking with her. For once, sleep came quickly and easily, with Fleur the last thing on his mind before he drifted off.

Sometime later, he sat bolt upright, his eyes straining to see through the darkness. His heart pounded in his chest and his breath came in gasps.

He began to shake, as if he could shake off the night terrors. What were these dreams trying to tell him?

Jeff had featured in his dreams of late, but tonight, Fleur had also appeared. He knew they most likely meant nothing, but he was uncomfortable with Fleur showing up in dreams where everyone died.

He raked a hand across his hair and exhaled hard. This was crazy thinking. Getting out of bed, he began pacing the room. Perhaps he should cancel seeing her. If seeing her was going to do this to him, it couldn't be healthy.

Then her words on the phone came back to him. *I don't know your earthly father, Callum, but I do know something. Your Heavenly Father only wants the best for you, with no conditions attached. He loves you unconditionally, and there's not a thing you can do or a medal you can be awarded that can earn it.*

Her calm assurance about God's unconditional love touched him deep down. He wasn't sure how that tied in with his dreams, but he stopped pacing and went over to the window and pulled the blind aside. It was a clear night, with the stars bright against the sky's inky backdrop. As he stared out at the heavens, a peace came over him that chased away the scene from his dream. Maybe he should go to church with her. Maybe there he'd find some answers.

CHAPTER 5

leur finished pinning her hair up as she glanced at the clock. Callum would be here in a few minutes, and her stomach was churning. She looked at Will and Lucy where they sat colouring at the table and wondered why she'd ever thought it was a good idea to have Callum meet her here. She'd thought it would be easier for him since he didn't know anyone else at the barbecue, but now she was worrying both what other people would think and how the children would respond to him. When she'd told them a friend who'd known their father was coming with them to Amy's, she'd worried about how they would react. Lucy had seemed vaguely interested, then forgot about it within ten minutes, whereas Will's little face had lit up like a Christmas tree.

"He knew my dad?" he said with a look of longing on his face that had broken Fleur's heart. Why hadn't she given it more thought? She wanted to warn Will not to bombard Callum with questions but hadn't had the heart. Instead she tried to distract them both, all the while growing more and more anxious herself.

The doorbell rang and she jumped. She took a deep breath and opened the door, offering a welcoming smile and hoping the fizzing nervousness didn't show.

"Hey." Callum grinned at her, almost shyly.

"Hey yourself." She let him in, trying not to stare. Having only ever seen him in gym gear and his uniform, the sight of him in perfectly fitting jeans and a tight white t-shirt that clung to his honed frame made her mouth suddenly go dry. She quickly led him into the kitchen, hoping he hadn't seen her reaction and chiding herself for acting like a schoolgirl.

Lucy and Will looked up with interest. Fleur introduced them, feeling awkward and sensing that Callum did also. Again, she wondered if this wasn't a terrible idea.

"Did you know my dad?" Will asked, bounding up to him. For a second, Fleur thought she sensed Callum flinch.

"Yes, I did," Callum replied warmly. "He was a great guy. You look a lot like him."

Will beamed proudly. "I know! Everyone says that. I'm writing about him. Well, sort of, for my homework project. Do you know much about military history?"

Callum chuckled and glanced briefly at Fleur. "Quite a bit, actually. In fact, I teach it. Maybe I can help you with your project."

"Oh, you don't have to do that," Fleur said quickly. "Will, stop pestering." Guilt assailed her when Will hung his head.

"It's fine," Callum assured her, bringing a smile back to Will's face.

As the two began chatting about Will's homework, Lucy let out an audible groan. "Boys," she said to no one in particular.

The two carried on chatting—or rather, Will bombarded Callum with questions and barely gave him time to answer one question before moving on to the next—throughout the car ride to Amy's house. Fleur found she was glad of the distraction. It felt odd, yet at the same time weirdly comfortable, to have Callum in her car, although she felt a little unsettled by how seamlessly he seemed to have become a part of her life in such a short time. She tried to remind herself that she was being a good friend and neighbour, and that was all.

Even so, she was relieved when they arrived at Amy's, although when Amy opened the door and made no secret of her blatant appraisal of Callum, Fleur felt herself cringe just a little on the inside.

"Well look at you, handsome," Amy said approvingly, winking at Fleur. "I've heard a lot about you."

"Really?" Callum glanced at Fleur, looking surprised but not displeased.

She felt her cheeks grow hot. "Yes, I was telling Amy about you being new to Salford. I'm sure there'll be lots of people here she'd love to introduce you to." Fleur glared at Amy over Will's shoulder as she steered the children inside.

Amy simply grinned. "Of course. Come through to the backyard," she said brightly.

Fleur hung back with the children as Amy introduced Callum to her husband, Angus, and a few of the guys from church. She didn't want people assuming they were a couple. Watching Callum begin to mingle, she was struck by how easily he seemed to get on with people, and yet at the same time there was an almost imperceptible aloofness to him, an unseen boundary. It was probably just his military training, but she didn't remember Jeff ever having that same quality. There was something about Callum that set him apart, and while it wasn't a bad thing, she thought again that he must be incredibly lonely.

As the afternoon wore on, the late summer sun beat down and Amy and Fleur were soon sitting in the shade enjoying fresh orange juice with soda while Angus laboured over the barbecue. Callum had offered to help and seemed to be genuinely enjoying himself. Watching him, Fleur felt Amy's eyes on her.

"He's nice," Amy said casually.

Fleur nodded. "Yes, he is."

"I was right about him being good-looking too, wasn't I?" Amy teased.

When Fleur didn't answer, Amy shook her head, laughing. "It is alright to notice, Fleur. You don't have to pretend men don't exist for the rest of your life."

Fleur snorted. "I notice men. I see them all the time at the gym. Callum's going through a rough time; I'm trying to be a friend."

"And that's all?"

"You're relentless! Yes, that's all," Fleur said firmly, her tone one that invited no further discussion of the matter.

Amy, of course, was determined to discuss it anyway. "Well, that's a shame," she said in a serious tone, "because you'd have to be blind not to see the way he looks at you."

Fleur faced her friend and frowned. "Really?"

"Yes," Amy said matter-of-factly, "and why wouldn't he?

You're a beautiful woman, and you can't be on your own forever. I don't believe for one moment that Jeff would want that."

Fleur fell silent. Then she nodded towards Callum. "He's not a Christian, so a relationship is out of the question for me. You know that."

"Give him time," Amy said softly.

As they continued to look over towards the barbecue, Callum glanced up. His gaze met Fleur's, and for a moment, something passed between them, a sudden connection sparking, a desire igniting. Fleur broke the gaze, suddenly feeling the need to fluff up her cushion.

Never one to miss anything, Amy took a thoughtful sip of her drink. "You must have caught the sun," she said nonchalantly, "your cheeks have gone pink."

IT WAS EARLY EVENING, the sun hovering just above the horizon and giving off a hazy heat when they drove back to Fleur's. Will was quiet this time, his eyelids heavy, and Lucy was engrossed in a book, though glancing in her rear-view mirror, Fleur saw her eyes fluttering, too. They would be straight to bed, she thought with a contented smile, feeling a rush of gratitude to God for her children and her friends and summer evenings like this. She glanced over at Callum, who smiled at her.

"Thank you for inviting me. I had a really good time. Your friends were really very welcoming."

"I'm glad," she said honestly. He'd fitted in so easily it was difficult to think that he hadn't met any of them before that afternoon. Jeff had spoken about his easy-to-get-on-with nature. Now she'd seen if for herself. As they pulled up outside her house there was an awkward pause, then she asked in a rush, "Would you like to come in for coffee?"

He smiled. "Sure. That sounds great." He climbed out of the car and helped carry her bags into the house.

Lucy headed straight upstairs to run a bath while Will raided the cupboard for chocolate.

"Not before bed, Will. You've had enough to eat. Go and get ready for bed."

The boy pouted before dragging his feet up the stairs. Pausing halfway up, he turned and looked down. "Hey Callum," he called out. As Callum looked up, Will stood smartly to attention and saluted. Callum laughed and saluted back. Will continued upstairs looking pleased with himself as Fleur chuckled to herself. "He's really taken with you."

"They're great kids," Callum said, following her into the kitchen.

Fleur busied herself with the coffeepot, feeling awkward again now that they were on their own. She remembered the look that had passed between them earlier and knew that as much as she tried to rationalise it away, the connection she'd felt in that moment couldn't be denied. Maybe she'd made a mistake inviting him in, but she couldn't ask him to leave now. That would be rude.

As she turned to ask how he took his coffee, she saw him staring at something on the wall and followed his gaze. On the corkboard where she kept school reports, to do lists and the kids' artwork, was an old photograph of her and Jeff. She was leaning on his shoulder, sticking her tongue out at the camera.

Callum was looking at it with an inscrutable expression on his face.

"That was when I was pregnant with Lucy," she said. The atmosphere had shifted, but to what she wasn't sure.

"You both look happy," Callum said, a wistfulness in his voice. He cleared his throat and turned away from the picture. When he spoke, it was in that formal voice he sometimes used, not meeting her gaze. "I think I'll leave the coffee. I'll be awake all night. But thanks for today."

"Oh, okay. That's fine." Although disappointed, she was also relieved. She walked him to the door, and after he thanked her once again, she watched him go with conflicting emotions warring inside her.

Halfway down the path, he turned around. "I was wondering...I meant to ask..."

"Yes?" Despite herself, she felt a leap of hope. His next words surprised her.

"Is it okay if I come to church with you on Sunday?"

"Of course!" She broke into a wide, open smile. "But it's probably best if you meet me there." She gave him directions and then watched as he got into his car while she sent up a prayer asking God to touch his heart. And to settle hers.

CHAPTER 6

*C*allum sat in his car outside the church, inspecting his nails while he waited for Fleur. He wasn't sure why he felt nervous. It wasn't like he'd never been to church before. The army held services on special occasions like Christmas and Easter. And he used to go as a child.

But meeting Fleur and listening to her talk about her faith had made him realise it could be so much more than that. Something that had always just been an occasional ritual, done because it was expected of him, was an entire way of life for her, the lens through which she saw the world. He hadn't come across that before.

Then at the barbecue, he'd met others with the same outlook. Besides that, he couldn't remember ever having felt so comfortable with a group of people he barely knew. He wanted what they had, although he wasn't sure exactly what that was.

Yet, he still felt nervous. There was part of him that felt almost unworthy. He knew others saw him as a hero, as an indisputably 'good' person, a role model. But he wasn't too sure that description was accurate.

As his nightmares continued to haunt him and his guilt continued to grow, he called his entire existence into question. Were the things he'd done really so noble? People had died. His marriage had broken down. What had been the point of it all?

He sat there growing more and more dejected until he spotted Fleur's car, and his heart leaped. She parked and climbed out, looking fresh and pretty in floral trousers and a simple shirt. She laughed as the kids pulled at her hands.

The kids. Meeting Will and Lucy had given him much food for thought. He'd missed out on so much by being alone for so long and making the army his entire purpose for living. At the same time, watching the longing in Will's eyes as he spoke about Jeff, Callum was sure he'd made the right decision to remain single after Danielle left. To bring children into the world when he'd be away from them for months at a time, would have been difficult. And the potential to be taken away from them forever? No, he was glad he hadn't taken that path.

It had been Jeff's path, though. When Callum's eyes had fallen on the photograph of him and Fleur on her kitchen board, he'd found himself overwhelmed by survivor's guilt. Here he was, standing in what should have been the man's kitchen, having spent the afternoon with his wife and children, while Jeff was...gone. Although he worried that his abrupt departure had seemed rude, he'd had no choice but to leave.

He continued to watch Fleur, psyching himself up to get out of the car to greet her, when she spotted him and waved. Will began to run over to the car, and Callum found himself grinning at the little boy, his worries momentarily forgotten.

He climbed out and smiled at Will. "Hey buddy. How's the project coming along?"

"It's great! I'm going to get an A for sure!"

"You don't know that, Will," Lucy admonished, coming up behind. She smiled at Callum. "Hello. Mum said you were coming."

"Yes. I haven't been to church in a long time and I thought it was time I did," he replied.

Lucy looked sympathetic. "It's quite boring really, the adults' bit. You can come into the children's club if you want. It's much better."

"Thank you, I might just do that." Callum chuckled at the child's complete honesty before Fleur reached them, shaking her head.

"Lucy! Stop putting him off before he even gets in there." She met his gaze and playfully rolled her eyes. "Hey," she said softly.

He smiled. "I'm sorry I left so abruptly the other evening," he began as they walked over to the church, the children running ahead.

"It's okay. I understand. It must have been an overwhelming day for you."

They reached the entrance and a slightly rotund man with a welcoming smile shook his hand.

"This is Pastor Tony," Fleur said, introducing him, "and this is Lieutenant Colonel Westaway."

"Just plain Callum's fine," he said quickly, pumping the man's hand. The pastor had a round, open face and eyes Callum felt held more wisdom than the guy's jolly demeanour announced at first glance.

Stepping inside, he took a seat next to Fleur and glanced around. He was used to traditional churches, which although beautiful, had always left him feeling a little intimidated as a child. This was a large, airy room with modern timber furniture and glass etchings on the wall. The altar was simple, though a large cross-shaped light installation hung behind it on the back wall, providing a dramatic focal point in the room. As he gazed at the cross, a quiet peace came over him, soothing his nerves.

The pastor stepped to the front of the church and said a few words before introducing the worship band. Callum was amazed to see young men and women with drums, a keyboard and an acoustic guitar set up in one corner.

"I wasn't expecting that," he murmured to Fleur as they stood.

She smiled at him and said, "They're great. I think you'll enjoy the music."

As the band began to play, the singer, a dark-haired young man with startlingly green eyes, announced the song with a quote from scripture. "The Word says, 'For the spirit of heaviness put on the garment of praise.'" He paused and looked around enthusiastically at the congregation. "Let's put on the garment of praise and worship God together."

He then began to sing those very words. His voice was raw, throaty, and filled with passion, and as he sang with his eyes closed, a look of rapture filled his face. Callum had not seen or heard anything like this before. It was certainly different from the old-fashioned hymns he was used to.

The congregation was obviously familiar with the song, and beside him, Fleur joined in with gusto. Although he felt a little awkward, Callum started mouthing the words and before he knew it, he found himself singing the refrain.

The next song gave him pause for thought. *'This is how I fight my battles... It may look like I'm surrounded but I'm surrounded by You...'*

He wasn't exactly sure what the words meant, yet the idea of a different way of fighting battles other than the way he knew, intrigued him.

As the song finished and he sat down, Fleur turned to him and smiled. "Are you doing okay?"

Nodding, he returned her smile. "Yes. I'm good, thanks."

He listened as the pastor read out the notices and then sent the children off to Sunday School. As she passed him, Lucy gave him a serious look. "Remember, you can join us if you get fed up. No one will mind."

"Thank you." Callum hid a chuckle and shared a smile with Fleur. "She's great. They both are," he said honestly.

Fleur grinned with pride and then nodded towards the front.

Callum settled in his seat as the pastor cleared his throat. He assumed this was the part where it would all go over his head and he should consider taking Lucy up on her offer, but as the pastor began speaking with a clear, strong voice, he sat attentively and listened.

"We're all fighting our own wars, aren't we? Wars of worry, anxiety, of never feeling good enough, our insatiable desire for material possessions, of struggling against injustice, and temptation, and sin. It can feel like the battle never stops."

The guy was right. That's how he felt. He wasn't on the

battlefield anymore, but the battle in his head hadn't stopped; in fact, it was growing worse.

"But as our song this morning tells us," the pastor continued, "as Christians, we're called to fight our battles a different way. We're not left to battle on our own. No, when we're surrounded on all sides, when we feel hemmed in and overwhelmed, we need to turn to God, because He is with us, no matter what we're going through, and He has the answers to all of life's problems."

He picked up his Bible. "Let's turn to first Corinthians chapter fifteen, verse fifty-seven." Fleur passed Callum a small paperback book with 'New Testament' on the cover. "They're free for visitors," she whispered. Callum took it gratefully and flipped through it. He had no idea where to find the right chapter but was too embarrassed to ask. Fleur found it for him and gave him a small smile.

He read along silently as the pastor read aloud.

"'But thanks be to God, who gives us the victory through our Lord Jesus Christ.' But how does He do this? We read in first John, chapter five, verse four, 'For everyone who has been born of God overcomes the world. And this is the victory that has overcome the world—our faith.'

"If you want victory against the world, against all the things that threaten to overwhelm you, you must turn to God, have faith, and be born again. Not physically, but spiritually. Allow God to transform your hearts and minds, and allow the fruit of the Spirit: love, joy, peace, patience, kindness, goodness, faithfulness, gentleness, and self-control, to infiltrate your lives. Let Jesus take His place as Lord of your life. He died that you might have life and have it to the full. If you're not experiencing that fullness, but are weighed down on every side, I'm here to tell you today that you can have it. You don't need to fight your battles alone. God is waiting to help you. All you need do is reach out to Him, and He'll be there.

"We might not admit it, but so much of our lives is consumed by revenge and jealousy. What we don't realise is that when we seek justice and revenge when people do us wrong, we're so often the ones who suffer. In Romans twelve we read, *'Bless those who persecute you; bless and do not curse. Rejoice with those who rejoice; mourn with those who mourn. Live in harmony with one another. Do not be proud but be willing to associate with people of low position. Do not be conceited.*

"'Do not repay anyone evil for evil. Be careful to do what is right in the eyes of everyone. If it is possible, as far as it depends on you, live at peace with everyone. Do not take revenge, my dear friends, but leave room for God's wrath, for it is written: "It is mine to avenge; I will repay," says the Lord. On the contrary: "If your enemy is hungry, feed him; if he is thirsty, give him something to drink. In doing this, you will heap burning coals on his head." Do not be overcome by evil, but overcome evil with good.'"

"It's not a natural human response to overcome evil with good, and yet, that's what God calls us to do. If we want victory in our lives, we need to start thinking differently, acting differently, responding differently. Jesus calls us to be different. To stand out. To be salt and light in this world that is consumed by hatred, greed and violence. That's my challenge to you today. How will you respond?"

Callum blinked. He'd not heard anything like this before. It was radical, yet somehow made sense, not that he understood it all. Maybe he should have gone with Lucy. But no, he was both intrigued and puzzled by the message.

All the battles he'd fought as a soldier had been of man's making. He knew that, but while he'd always been on the side of justice, the futility of the way mankind tried to solve its problems swept over him. *Was there really another way? A better way?*

All the slaughter, carnage and destruction he'd seen over many years could have been avoided if mankind had chosen a different way. God's way. He was shocked to find himself fighting back tears. He never cried.

Soldiers didn't cry.

He straightened in his seat and regained his composure, then he felt a warm touch on his hand as Fleur's fingers brushed against his as she somehow sensed his distress. Before he could think about it, he placed his hand over hers. They sat that way for a few moments as the pastor continued with his sermon, although now Callum was distracted by the feel of Fleur's skin on his. It was as though an electrical current ran from her hand to his, energising him, and he was acutely aware of her physical proximity in a way that was simultaneously comforting and disturbing. He didn't know whether he was relieved or disappointed when the pastor asked them to pick up their bibles again and Fleur dropped his hand without meeting his eyes.

The pastor finished by reading from Colossians chapter one. *"'Since, then, you have been raised with Christ, set your hearts on things above, where Christ is, seated at the right hand of God. Set your minds on things above, not on earthly things.'"* His final sentence rang in Callum's thoughts. *"Where your treasure is, there your heart will be also."*

What did he treasure? For so long it had been his army career, his medals, his ability to get the job done and organise his men. However, any pleasure or real pride he took in his position and the status that came with it had been lost long ago. He didn't feel he had anything to treasure; for a long time, life had been only about going through the motions.

He wanted more than that.

As the pastor ended his sermon and everyone bowed their heads to pray, Callum found himself doing the same, but instead of listening to the pastor, he prayed his own silent prayer: *Please, God, if You're truly there, help me to find You. I'm tired of fighting.*

The service ended, and as they rose to their feet, Fleur asked if he'd enjoyed it.

He wasn't so sure 'enjoy' was the right word, but he said he had, anyway. "I'm glad I came." He glanced down at the small New Testament in his hand.

"You can keep that." Their gazes met, and warmth filled him as he recalled the way they'd briefly held hands. Intensity simmered between them, but he wondered if either of them was ready to face their growing attraction. He cleared his throat and opened his mouth to say something when a woman's voice distracted them both and Fleur looked away.

"Hello, darling!" The woman, a smaller, older version of Fleur, rushed up to them and rubbed Fleur's arm. "Your father and I were late, and we had to sit at the back." She glanced at Callum and then back at Fleur. "Are you going to introduce me?"

Fleur smiled, although she looked a little embarrassed. "Mum, this is Lieutenant...'

"It's Callum," he cut in, leaning forward and shaking Fleur's mother's hand.

She nodded at him approvingly, while her gaze travelled over him. "Pleased to meet you. I'm Lydia. I don't think I've seen you before. Are you new to town?"

"Yes. I'm working at the barracks as a trainer."

"Well, you're very welcome. I hope Fleur's been looking after you." She raised a brow and looked towards her daughter pointedly.

Callum chuckled. "Yes, she's been great."

Lydia frowned, angling her head. "So, how do you know each other?"

Both he and Fleur hesitated a moment before Fleur answered quickly, "Callum was Jeff's commanding officer."

Lydia inhaled deeply. "Well, I'm pleased you've befriended each other." She rubbed Fleur's arm again. "I was going to ask if you and the children would like to come for a spot of lunch. Your father's made your favourite lemon cake. Why don't you bring Callum with you?"

"Er..." Before Fleur could reply, Lydia nodded as though the matter was settled and turned towards Will and Lucy who were trotting towards them.

"I see where Lucy gets her forthrightness from," Callum whispered to Fleur, grinning.

"You mean bossiness," Fleur said with a giggle. "Anyway, would you like to come?"

"I'm not sure I should. I think I'd be intruding."

"You wouldn't be." Her gaze was steady and sent a small tremor through his body.

"Okay," he said, "I'd love to."

FLEUR LOOKED out the window to watch her father, Callum, Will and Lucy playing rounders on the lawn. They were all getting on like a house on fire. It was funny, she mused, but Callum seemed to fit seamlessly in with her family and friends as though she'd known him for years.

"He's very nice," her mother said from behind. "A good choice."

"Mum! You're as bad as Amy. He's just a friend."

"Friends don't look at each other the way you two were looking at each other at church."

Fleur sighed. There was no point in arguing; she knew her mother was right. As much as she'd repeatedly tried to deny it, her feelings for Callum were becoming more complicated by the day. She wanted to be his friend, wanted to help him along his journey to God if he wished to continue with it, but she couldn't keep kidding herself that was all it was. The look that had passed between them at church...Fleur knew exactly what her mother meant.

"What's holding you back, darling?" Her mother put an arm around Fleur's shoulders, her tone gentle.

Fleur shrugged. "The kids, for one. I can't afford to make mistakes."

"Of course. But they seem so good together."

Fleur nodded.

"But it's not just that, is it?"

Fleur watched Will squeal in delight as he made it all the way around the lawn before his granddad managed to catch the ball. "No. Although he came to church this morning, he's not a Christian. There's no way I can date him."

Her mother looked crestfallen and patted her hand. "I didn't know. I'm sorry."

"There's nothing to be sorry about, Mum. As you said, you didn't know."

"If he came to church, he must be seeking."

Fleur nodded. "I think so, but he's a bit mixed up at the moment."

"Mixed up is fine. God can help him sort things out, we know that. And there's no harm in being friends, but I agree, you shouldn't consider dating him at the moment, which is a pity, because he seems so nice."

Fleur winced. "I know."

Shortly after, the children ran into the kitchen with her dad and Callum close behind.

"They've worn me out," Callum said, laughing. He looked so happy and relaxed compared to when they'd met just a few weeks earlier. She bit her lip. It would be so easy to fall for him, but she couldn't allow herself to go down that path. She'd seen what happened to her friend, Lisa, when she'd married an unbeliever. The struggles she and her husband, Tim, had gone through when they discovered they wanted different things. Their priorities had not been the same and it simply didn't work. The instructions Jesus had given to not be unequally yoked had been given for a reason.

A while later, she walked him to his car while Will and Lucy said their goodbyes to their grandparents. It was hard not to be drawn to him, but she'd resolved to only be friends, nothing more.

They stopped when they reached his car and faced each other. Fleur tried to hide her conflicted emotions and smiled brightly. "It's been great spending time with you today. Do you think you'll come to church again next week?"

"Definitely. I don't claim to understand it all, but I really felt something today. Thank you," he said, looking deep into her eyes.

She swallowed hard. "What for?"

"I would never have thought to go to church if I hadn't met you. And for showing me around, introducing me to people...you've really helped me settle in."

She gave him an appreciative smile. "It's been a pleasure."

He shifted his weight from one foot to the other. "I...I was wondering if you fancied lunch again this week?"

A small breath slipped from the corner of her mouth. How could she refuse without being rude? Was having lunch inviting trouble, or could she spend time with him and remain strong in her resolve? Maybe he only wanted her as a friend as well. She couldn't deny him that, could she? "Okay. I'd love to," she said honestly.

"Great!" His face lit up and she thought how boyish he looked, completely different to the stoic Lt Cl. He smiled and promised to call. She held her breath when she thought he might kiss her, but let it out when he didn't. He got into his car and waved as he drove away, and she once again offered up a prayer for him. And for herself.

CHAPTER 7

*C*allum sat bolt upright, gasping for air. The dream again, and once more, Fleur was in it. He stumbled to the bathroom and splashed water over his face, taking deep breaths to give his heart time to calm down.

He had to talk to someone about this. As much as he didn't want to admit it, he was clearly suffering a form of PTSD. He'd seen it happen to a few of his men over the years and been the first to tell them it was nothing to be ashamed of and they needed to ask for help.

But it was never supposed to happen to him.

Trudging back to his bedroom, he glanced at the flashing number on his alarm clock. It was due to go off in an hour—there was no point in going back to sleep. He turned the light on and sat down on his bed, his gaze falling on the book next to the clock. The New Testament Fleur had given him at church.

He picked it up, flicked to one of the passages the pastor

had been reading and carried on from there. At first, he didn't understand what he was reading, but as he continued, a picture started to build in his mind and he felt he was beginning to figure out what the message of Jesus was all about.

Growing up, it had just been about the traditions of Christmas and Easter and keeping the Ten Commandments, but now he began to realise what he'd missed. The message of love, justice and peace rang true to him, and as he read further about Jesus' betrayal and journey to the cross, he felt the emotion of the story, feeling a lifting in his heart when he read Luke's account of the resurrection. He'd always taken his parents' religion for granted and been happy enough to ascribe it to himself, but he had never truly believed or understood. It had seemed like old traditions that had no relevance to him. But now, he was beginning to see why Fleur had thrown her heart and soul into her faith.

But could he be a Christian like she was? Could he devote his life to God? He was a soldier, not a chaplain. Where did his career in defence fit into this message of love and forgiveness? He'd been called to fight, to kill if necessary, not to love and forgive.

He put the New Testament down just as his alarm sounded, a shrill note cutting through the quiet of the morning. He got up and started to get ready, trying to focus his thoughts on the day ahead.

All morning, though, he struggled, his thoughts returning to the things he'd heard and read, trying to make sense of it all. After Military History, when he'd dismissed the recruits for lunch, he looked up from his desk to see Billy Cassidy hovering in the doorway. He frowned at the lad. "Something wrong, Cassidy?"

The lad looked uncomfortable, staring at his feet. "Can I have a word, sir?"

Callum felt a rush of empathy for the youth and wondered what was troubling him. "Of course. Sit down." He nodded to a chair opposite. Billy sat and looked at his hands.

"What is it, son?" Callum asked.

"The thing is, sir, I don't know if this is for me."

Callum's brows lifted in surprise. It was the last thing he'd expected to hear. Contrary to Jarrop's expectations, Billy was their sharpest and finest recruit. His troubled background lent him an astuteness and street smarts that would serve him well.

"Are you missing your old life, Cassidy? I appreciate it must be quite an adjustment."

Billy shook his head vehemently. "Not at all, sir. Joining the forces is the best decision I've ever made—I'd be in jail otherwise, I know that. It's just...I don't want to kill people. I don't want it to be about that. Otherwise I may as well go back to the gang. What's the difference, really?"

Callum leaned back in his chair, not sure how to respond. The boy could have no idea about his own recent struggles, couldn't know that his words hit him like a sledgehammer. He was deciding how to answer when Billy spoke again.

"I wanted to know if I could be a doctor instead, sir? For the army, like. Instead of going for infantry. Believe it or not I passed my high school exams; I was really good at science, too. I could do it. I know I could."

Absorbing Billy's words, Callum studied him thoughtfully, steepling his hands in front of him. "It's certainly possible.

You're still in basic training, so there's still a window for you to rethink your trade. You'd have to pass another entrance exam for medical training, but yes, I'm happy to put you forward for it. I'll have to get clearance, but I think you've got a good shot at being accepted. You've proven yourself over the past few weeks, Cassidy. If you're sure that's what you want and you're prepared to put the work in, then you've got my backing."

Billy's face lit up like all his Christmases had come at once, and Callum realised how young the lad really was.

"Thank you, sir, thank you!"

"It's fine. Now, run along, I've got things to do."

Billy nodded, saluted and dashed off. Callum stared after him. He felt relieved at Billy's decision. Of course, being an army doctor was often as dangerous as being a soldier, but the boy had an obvious calling and it was a more noble use of his skills.

And it would spare him the guilt and memories of horror that Callum lived with on a daily basis. As he thought about Billy, and himself, and tried not to think of Fleur, he made a split-second decision.

He would talk to the chaplain.

As he knocked on the door, he glanced around to make sure no one saw him. After all, everyone knew that unless you had a devoted faith, the only time anyone went to see the chaplain was if they were struggling. He didn't want Jarrop, especially, to know how he was feeling.

The chaplain, a slight man with warm grey eyes, looked up in surprise as Callum came into his office. "Lieutenant Colonel? Can I help?"

"Call me Callum," Callum said wearily, standing in front of the chaplain's desk, feeling awkward.

The chaplain angled his head and nodded. "Of course. And you can call me John. Take a seat. What can I do for you?"

Callum realised he had no idea what he wanted to say or how to begin the conversation. He rubbed his hand across his forehead and sat, wondering where to start. He ended up talking about Billy.

When he finished, the chaplain looked thoughtful. "It sounds as though you've been a good source of guidance for the boy, and that he's come to understand the calling God has placed on his heart. Admirable at such a young age and from the background you describe. But if you don't mind me saying so, Lieutenant...Callum...I get the feeling that this isn't the real reason you're here." The chaplain's voice was kind, but his words hit home.

"No, I don't suppose it is. I need some...guidance. I've met this woman. Not just any woman, a widow. Jeff Gibbons' widow. And I went to church, and the sermon was about priorities. And living a different way. The men I've seen die, the enemies I've killed...but Jesus tells us to love our enemies...and I'm getting these nightmares..." His voice trailed off. He was rambling and not making any sense. "I'm sorry," he said miserably. "I shouldn't have come."

"Not at all. But maybe you could start at the beginning."

Callum gave a small chuckle, and then, hesitantly at first, told the other man about the feelings that had been building in him for a long time that had led him to take the training post here at Salford. He also spoke of issues causing him to consider his options for the future. While staring at his hands in shame, he told him about the nightmares. He told him about Fleur, and Jeff. And finally, he told him about church and the peace he'd momentarily felt, and about reading the gospel of Luke that morning. When he finished, he felt exhausted.

John looked at him with compassion. "This is a really troubling time, isn't it? But I get the sense that God is reaching out to you."

Callum frowned. "Why would God want to reach out to me? I've done such terrible things."

"Because He loves you. As simple as that. God doesn't condemn you, Callum. You did what you did in the name of justice, and you believed you were doing the right thing. Who knows how many lives have been saved through your interventions? This guilt you feel, perhaps it's a sign you need to throw yourself on God's mercy. After all, none of us come to Him through pride. God loves a humble heart."

Could that be true? Did he need to throw himself onto God's mercy? Turn to God like the pastor had said? But wasn't that a sign of weakness? Did it matter? It was all too much. "You're saying that God can free me of all of this?"

"Yes. Although I'd suggest you seek counselling as well. I think you're experiencing the after-effects of trauma as well as being spiritually awakened. PTSD they call it these days. There's no shame in that. You're a human, not a machine. It's usually a case of having been too strong for too long."

Callum chewed his lip while drumming the arm of his chair with his fingertips. "I'll think about it."

"Good. In the meantime, I suggest you read the gospel of John. Come back when you're ready to talk about everything further."

Callum stood to leave. "Thank you. I will."

The chaplain stood at the same time. "Could I pray for you before you leave?"

Callum stiffened. No one had ever offered to do that before. "Er... I guess so."

John stepped around his desk and placed a hand lightly on Callum's shoulder. Although it felt strange, it also felt kind of comforting. His voice was quiet as he began to pray. "Lord God, I pray for my brother. He's confused and hurting, but he's also seeking. Reveal Yourself to him, I pray. Let him grasp how wide and long and high and deep the love of Christ is for him, and let him know this love that surpasses knowledge— that he might be filled to the measure of all the fullness of God. May his life be transformed by Your love. In Jesus' precious name. Amen."

THAT EVENING, Callum sat at his kitchen table and opened his New Testament to the gospel of John, like the chaplain had suggested. As before, he didn't fully understand what he was reading, although he grasped it was truth and held the message of life that he'd been missing but was now seeking. When he reached chapter three, verses sixteen to twenty-one spoke directly to him.

'For God so loved the world that He gave His one and only Son, that whoever believes in Him shall not perish but have eternal life. For God did not send His Son into the world to condemn the world, but to save the world through him.

Whoever believes in Him is not condemned, but whoever does not believe stands condemned already because they have not believed in the name of God's one and only Son. This is the verdict: Light has come into the world, but people loved darkness instead of light because their deeds were evil. Everyone who does evil hates the light and will not come into the light for fear that their deeds will be exposed. But whoever lives by the truth comes into the light, so that it may be seen plainly that what they have done has been done in the sight of God.'

As he re-read the verses, this time aloud, he felt his heart shift and knew for a certainty that God's sacrificial love surpassed anything he'd ever known.

He closed the book, and bowing his head, clasped his hands. "Dear God, I don't deserve Your love. I still don't fully understand it, but I want to. Please show me the way. Show me what I need to do, because right now, I feel lost." The image of Fleur came to him, and the comforting touch of her hand in his. "Keep her safe, Lord, even if she's not meant for me. I want her to be happy. I feel so guilty about Jeff, although I know deep down his death wasn't my fault. She deserves happiness." He brushed his eyes and inhaled slowly.

As he settled himself for the night and prepared for bed, his prayers echoed in his heart with expectancy.

That night, he had another dream. Not the same dream he'd been having. In this one, a man, swarthy and Middle Eastern, walked towards him, holding out his hand. A stillness radiated from him that seemed to disrupt the very air around him. As he approached and Callum looked into the man's eyes and saw the love and compassion that radiated from within, he gasped and knew instantly who He was.

Shocked, Callum was unable to move until the man reached him and held out a hand. "Come, Callum."

"You know my name?"

He smiled. "Of course. I've known you since before you were born. We've always known each other; you'd just forgotten. Take my hand."

Callum took His hand and stood to his feet, trembling as he came eye to eye with his Lord and Saviour, too filled with awe to speak.

"Follow me."

Opening his eyes, Callum waited for the panic to hit.

It didn't come.

Instead, he felt as if he were held in a warm, loving embrace. Tears dampened his cheeks, but he didn't feel sad. He bowed his head and prayed. "Lord God, I want to follow You. Thank You for pursuing me." Snuggling into his blankets, he drifted into the most restful sleep he'd ever had. The nightmares had ended.

CHAPTER 8

allum met with the chaplain the day after his dream and committed his life to Christ. In the days following, it was as though a whole new dimension of the world had revealed itself to him, and he began to think about everything differently. While he was still struggling with his memories of war, things were becoming easier, and there'd been no more nightmares. He hadn't given any more thought to seeking counselling for his PTSD. He felt he didn't need it—God was healing him.

The change in his life felt like a miracle. Of course, according to the chaplain, God, being the creator of all things, knew all about miracles.

Giving his life to Christ had felt much like a rebirth. In that moment, as he'd completely surrendered to God and to God's will for him, whatever that would prove to be, he'd felt a sensation like a cool breeze rush through him, as if cleansing him of all his anxieties. He hadn't healed overnight, but he knew the process had begun, and he felt something he had never felt before—trust in something greater than himself.

Before he'd prayed, John had given him a piece of scripture from Acts seventeen to read that had stayed with him and he'd read it every day since.

"The God who made the world and everything in it is the Lord of heaven and earth and does not live in temples built by human hands. And He is not served by human hands, as if He needed anything. Rather, He Himself gives everyone life and breath and everything else. From one man He made all the nations, that they should inhabit the whole earth; and He marked out their appointed times in history and the boundaries of their lands. God did this so that they would seek Him and perhaps reach out for Him and find Him, though He is not far from any one of us. 'For in Him we live and move and have our being."

The message that mankind was made by God and for God, and nothing happened without Him, hit Callum with stunning clarity. He had indeed reached out for God and discovered He'd been right there all along, and now he felt he was coming to grasp the meaning of the words *'In Him we live and move and have our being.'* Now he understood the light he'd noticed in Fleur's eyes at that first meeting. God lived in her.

After they'd discussed the scripture together, John looked him in the eye and asked, "Are you ready?"

"Yes." He'd never felt so ready in his life.

John placed his hand gently on his shoulder as Callum bowed his head and began to pray the prayer John had given him to learn for just this moment.

"Lord Jesus," he began, "I believe You are the Son of God and You came from heaven to suffer and die on the cross for me. I believe that You rose from the dead and You are alive, and You are Lord of the universe. I confess that I've sinned against You and against people, and now I turn away from my sins and I look to You. You paid the penalty of my sins by giving up Your life for me. Now, I give my life to You, please live Your life in me."

As he confessed his sins, he thought about everything he'd been through and everything he'd done in his time in the army. Tears pricked his eyes, but soon dried as a sense of wonder filled his heart and he continued to pray.

"Please give me the faith to believe and live the promises You've written in Your Word, the Holy Bible. Give me the strength and the faith to accomplish the plans and the destiny You have for me and give me the courage to be a witness for You. Fill me with Your love and compassion for people so I can be like You. I pray all these things in Jesus' name. Amen."

After he finished, Callum sat in silence for some time, absorbing the moment. When he raised his head, the chaplain embraced him. "God bless you and keep you, Lieutenant Colonel."

When he told Fleur the news during lunch the following day, she was overwhelmed with joy. "That's fantastic, Callum. I'm so happy for you." Her smile was genuine and her eyes glistened with joy. They discussed the verses in Acts that John had given him to read and agreed to meet regularly to discuss other passages. "I'd invite you to my ladies' Bible study group, but you might feel out of place," she'd said with a laugh.

"You might be right." He laughed with her.

Over the following weeks, they saw each other regularly, at least every few days when they could fit time in around their work schedules, and he had spent several afternoons with the children. It had surprised him at first, but he was growing fond of Will and Lucy. He felt protective towards them and was genuinely interested when Fleur told him how they were getting on at school, or about funny things they'd said that day.

During their time together, they chatted about his newfound faith and how it translated into real life. He attended church regularly and was getting to know some of the church folk.

His weekly meetings with the chaplain were helping. John had pointed out to him that perhaps Fleur had been brought into his life for a reason, and that sometimes God brought the unlikeliest of people together. As Callum's newly forged relationship with God had deepened, all other relationships seemed to be deepening as well. He'd even had a pleasant phone conversation with his father and had told him and his mother, briefly, about Fleur. Of course it had been premature; his mother had gotten all excited and invited them both for dinner. He asked her to invite them again in a few weeks. If he was going to take Fleur to meet his parents, it would be when they were a real couple.

He hoped that would happen, and that it would be soon. Today, even. After weeks of being 'just friends' when it was so obvious that they both had feelings for each other, he knew it was time to have that conversation with her.

He wanted to do things properly, but as he drove to her house, his stomach was clenched tight and his hands were clammy on the wheel. He knew his feelings for Fleur were strong; this wasn't just a passing attraction.

It was happening fast, but he was starting to feel they were a family of sorts, and though he still felt a pang of guilt when he thought of Jeff, he had started to accept the situation as it was.

He pulled up outside her house, a neat, well-kept two-storey dark brick home. It was early afternoon. They both had a few hours away from work and the children were at school, so they'd arranged to meet for coffee. It was so natural now, to just arrange to see each other, as if they'd been friends for years.

He picked up the bunch of flowers he'd bought on the way, a lovely mix of colourful daisies and carnations, and walked up her drive, taking a deep breath as he knocked on the door.

After several seconds, the door opened, and Fleur stood there, looking as beautiful as ever. She gave a small gasp of delight when he presented her with the bunch of flowers. "Thank you. They're gorgeous."

"So are you," he said without thinking. Her lips parted in surprise, then her cheeks grew pink. She looked adorable. He swallowed hard.

"Well, thank you again." She gave him a smile that sent a tingle up his spine. "Would you like to come in?"

He nodded and followed her into the kitchen and watched as she arranged the flowers in a vase. When she turned to him, he stepped forward and took her hands. It was now or never. Her eyes widened but she didn't pull away.

"Fleur, I want to tell you something." He swallowed hard and gazed into her eyes. "I'm sure you know I have feelings for you. I'd love for us to pursue a relationship together, but I completely understand if you don't feel the same or aren't ready. If that's the case, I hope we can still be friends, and I promise I'll never mention it again. I'm your friend regardless, and I'll always be here for you and the children."

He stopped, amazed but relieved that he'd finally had the courage to give voice to his feelings. He may be decorated for valour but pouring out one's heart to a woman required a different kind of bravery altogether.

She stared at him. He thought he saw a fleeting glimpse of happiness twinkle in her eyes, but then they watered and she abruptly dropped his hands and turned her back to him before placing her palms on the counter. She didn't speak.

His heart sank. He'd gotten it all wrong. "Fleur?" The seconds that passed felt like hours as he waited for her to say something. He wanted to step to her and put his arms around her, but he didn't dare.

When she didn't answer, he drew a slow breath and turned to leave. The bottom had just dropped out of his world. It had been too soon. She didn't want him.

Only as he reached the front door did he hear her quietly calling his name.

CALLUM'S ADMISSION STUNNED HER, although part of her had been waiting for it. Hoping for it, even. He'd become a fixture in her life the last few weeks, and she'd no longer been able to deny the way her heart lifted and her body tingled every time she saw him. They'd laughed together, confided in each other, and talked about everything under the sun.

The revelation that he'd committed his life to the Lord had

thrilled her. He'd continued to come to church and she'd watched with joy as he'd started to grow in his faith.

But the second revelation, now that it had come, had shaken her to the core. She didn't understand what it was that was holding her back, the fear that curled in the pit of her stomach even as her heart leapt with joy at his words. She'd felt like sobbing with an emotion she couldn't name and had turned away rather than have him see her break down and think that he'd done something wrong.

Then she heard him quietly make his way towards the front door and she knew she couldn't let him leave. "Callum," she called softly.

He turned around, and she walked to him while brushing the tears that trickled down her cheeks.

"I've upset you," he said, looking distraught.

She shook her head. "No. Well, yes, but not in the way you mean."

She saw the hope in his face. "You mean...?"

She nodded. "I feel the same way, Callum. I'm just...scared, I suppose. It's been a long time; there's been no one since Jeff."

He lifted a hand to her face and stroked her cheek. She turned her face into the palm of his hand, acknowledging how right it felt. "I understand," he said. "As much as I hate to admit it, it's scary for me too. But I want you to know I'd never try to replace Jeff, not for you, nor for Lucy or Will. I respect what he was to you all, and I'll always respect his memory."

"Thank you." Her heart warmed and she smiled. He was such a gentleman, a rare diamond, just like Jeff had been. God had been good, giving her two such wonderful men.

But again, a shadow of fear caused her heart to palpitate.

She tried to rationalise it away. Of course she was nervous. She'd been on her own a long time and had the children to think of too.

They stood like that for a few moments, their gazes locked. Her heart pounded as she tried to throttle the dizzying current racing through her body. His lips were so close, she could almost taste them. Feel them.

The kettle whistled, interrupting the moment. She released a breath. Maybe it was for the best. "Come on, I'll make us some coffee." She took his hand and led him to the kitchen.

She made their drinks and then they sat in her sunroom, a pleasant but slightly awkward silence between them until she said, "I like you very much Callum, but I have Will and Lucy to consider. We'll need to take things slowly, and it might be best not to say anything to them for a while."

"Of course." Callum put down his coffee and picked up her hand, tracing his thumb around her palm. "I understand. I'll never push you, Fleur. You said slowly, so it'll be snail's pace unless you tell me otherwise."

She laughed at that, but also felt a rush of gratitude and again thanked God for bringing this man into her life. He respected her and would respect her boundaries. Although as she looked at him, the longing to be held by him, to be kissed by him, was almost too much.

They chatted for a while about their work, and about Amy's latest escapades, and Callum told her about the invitation to his parents' home one weekend, which she accepted, flattered they wanted to meet her so soon. Then Callum said he had to return to work, leaving her simultaneously disappointed and relieved. She loved spending time with him, but she also needed time alone to process what had just happened.

She walked him to the door, and as he left, he put a hand gently on her waist, leaned in and kissed her cheek. She closed her eyes as his lips brushed her skin.

"I'll call you later," he said in a soft voice as he left. When she closed the door behind him, she raised a hand to her cheek as a tumble of confused thoughts and feelings assailed her. She'd longed for this moment for weeks, but now that it had come, there was still that nagging fear, a feeling she didn't want to go near but also knew she couldn't keep running from.

Was it Jeff holding her back? Not wanting to let go of him?

She went upstairs and pulled a box from under her bed. It contained photos of them both, a necklace Jeff had bought her, an old Bible they'd read together and a few other keepsakes. Smiling to herself, she looked through them. She felt the pang of grief she always did, but there was a new lightness now, and the guilt she'd been feeling over her budding relationship with Callum had lessened.

It felt too right not to be part of God's plan. She knew Jeff would want her and the children to be happy and safe. So why all the inner turmoil? Why the fear at the depth of her feelings for Callum?

She picked up the Bible she'd shared with Jeff and allowed it to fall open in front of her.

Psalm thirty. She read the passage from the Passion translation with tears in her eyes.

O Lord, my healing God,
I cried out for a miracle and You healed me...

We may weep through the night but at daybreak it will turn into
shouts of ecstatic joy...
He has torn the veil and lifted from me the sad heaviness of
mourning.
He wrapped me in the glory garments of gladness.
How could I be silent when it's time now to praise You?
Now my heart sings out loud, bursting with joy—a bliss inside that
keeps me singing.
I can never thank You enough!

She prayed through the psalm slowly, taking in its message, then thanked God with a grateful heart that He had replaced her mourning with dancing. Wiping away her tears, she put the box back in its place and went downstairs and picked up the phone, a grin now on her face.

She just had to tell Amy.

CHAPTER 9

$\mathcal{A}$s Fleur glanced at Callum, her heart swelled with pride. Dashingly handsome in his formal uniform, she still couldn't quite believe they were now officially an item. Accompanying him to this, the Officers' annual Gala Ball, and being introduced as his girlfriend, filled her with an almost territorial feeling.

Over the last few weeks, since he'd taken her hands in the kitchen and confessed his feelings, they'd grown closer and closer. The beauty of taking things slowly on the physical side was that the emotional intimacy developed first. Jeff had been her childhood sweetheart and they'd grown up together, so there'd never been a time when she hadn't known him. With Callum, she was learning something new every day, and what was developing between them had a more mature, richer quality about it.

Even if right now she did feel as giddy as a schoolgirl.

He looked down at her and loped an arm around her waist. "Are you enjoying yourself?"

She looked up and smiled. "Yes." It was a glamorous affair, if a little stuffy, with a brass band that seemed terribly dated, but she wouldn't want to be anywhere else right now. She leaned into his side. "Are you?"

He laughed. "This year I am, because you're with me. Usually if I'm not away on tour when these things are on, I do everything I can to get out of them." His face showed obvious pride. "I've never brought anyone before."

She felt herself colour at that, feeling pleased. Although she felt no jealousy over his ex-wife, it was still nice to know this was a new experience for him too. "Do we have to come every year?" she whispered.

"I can't think of anything worse," he replied, chuckling.

Fleur giggled at that and took a sip of her sparkling apple juice.

Another couple approached them, and Callum's stoic officer face returned as he introduced Fleur. She noticed how respectful the young man was towards Callum as a senior officer and felt that glow of pride again. It had been clear all evening that anyone who knew Callum thought highly of him. Although he spoke to her about the army, this was a side of him that she hadn't seen. Of course, she knew that army life was rarely this glamorous, and being an army wife less so. She was glad that Callum was based at Salford and seemed happy about giving up active service. She knew he still felt conflicted about his role in training new recruits, but she also saw how much satisfaction he got from teaching them and watching them grow. It was one of the things she loved about him.

With her glass halfway to her mouth, she paused.

One of the things she loved about him?

Did she love him? Instantly, she knew the answer was yes. She was falling for him deeply, and while neither of them had said the words or discussed their future in any detail because she was still being tentative around the children, she was almost certain he felt the same. She thanked God for the blessing He'd brought into her life every day.

Watching Callum grow closer to the Lord even as their own relationship blossomed and grew was another blessing. He'd thrown himself into developing his faith, attending church with her on Sundays, and he'd also joined the men's Bible study group. He also continued to meet with the army chaplain once a week, and that seemed to be helping him process his conflicted feelings around his past. Fleur personally thought he should see a trauma counsellor, but that was a truth Callum would come to in his own time. God would guide him, as He had always guided her.

The evening wore on, and as much as she enjoyed being there with him, Fleur found herself relieved when the night came to a close. As they strolled back to Callum's car, she tipped her head back, relishing the cool breeze on her face after the stuffiness of the hall. After a moment, she felt Callum's gaze on her and looked sideways at him, a smile dancing on her lips. "What?"

His face reddened at getting caught staring at her. "I was just thinking how beautiful you are. I'm an incredibly lucky man. I felt so proud to be with you tonight."

She smiled. "I feel the same about you."

He took her hand and raised it to his lips.

Her heart was bubbling with joy. Should she tell him how she felt? Seizing the moment, she opened her mouth to do just that, when a booming voice sounded from behind them.

"Westaway! How are you?"

They both turned, and Callum nodded respectfully at the large, jowly man who approached with a stagger. Although he didn't have to salute at the gala, Callum automatically straightened. "Colonel Jarrop, sir."

The man reached them. His cheeks were red and his eyes bleary. If she wasn't mistaken, Colonel Jarrop had been partaking in a few too many glasses of champagne.

Fixing his eyes on her, he slurred, "And who's this, Westaway? Your lady?"

Callum nodded, smiling proudly at Fleur. "It is indeed, sir. Fleur, this is Colonel Jarrop."

Fleur held out her hand and the colonel pumped it. "Very pretty. Well done, Westaway. Very well done."

Fleur bit her lip and stifled another giggle.

"Thank you, sir," Callum replied, not sounding particularly amused. Jarrop turned and staggered back towards the hall.

"Is he usually like that?" she asked.

"No." Callum shook his head and sighed. "He's a character, but, no...I think he's had a few too many."

As they began walking towards the car again, they stopped when Callum's name was called again. "Westaway! I nearly forgot. I need you to come by my office in the morning."

Frowning, Callum nodded before leading Fleur to the car.

"What was that about?" she asked as she clipped her seatbelt on.

"No idea. Guess I'll find out tomorrow."

"AT EASE, LIEUTENANT COLONEL."

Callum relaxed and held his hands together behind his back. Jarrop had returned to his usual sterner, sober self. Callum had come straight to his office as requested, wondering what his commanding officer wanted of him. He hoped Billy hadn't gotten himself into some sort of trouble. The lad was still waiting to hear about his application for medical training and Callum knew he was growing frustrated.

"I've got news, Westaway, which may come as a shock. You've settled in well here, so it will be a shame to lose an educator of your calibre."

"Sir?" Foreboding curled in his gut.

"There's been a situation in Iraq. Your old platoon. You're being recalled for six months."

The room swam before his eyes. Panic assailed him. *No. No, no, no. Not again, not now. Fleur.* His thoughts scattered into fear filled fragments.

Jarrop frowned at him. "Everything alright, Westaway?"

"Yes, sir," Callum lied. He clasped his hands tighter behind his back, disgusted with himself to feel them trembling. Jarrop peered at him intently.

"Is there a *problem*, Westaway?" Jarrop barked. Callum shook his head no. There was no way he was going to admit to the colonel that he suspected he was struggling with PTSD, and that the thought of active duty filled him with terror. Jarrop was old school. Like Callum's father, he thought such things were a sign of weakness.

"Just a shock, sir."

"Yes, yes. No doubt you don't want to leave your new lady, eh?" Jarrop chuckled.

"Yes sir, that's it." Callum felt as though his words were coming from somewhere far away, as if he wasn't currently inhabiting his body. He tried to pray, but his thoughts were so scattered he couldn't connect. He had to get out of there. "When do I leave, sir?"

"Next Friday."

A week. He had a week. He was taking Fleur to meet his parents tomorrow, and they were discussing the possibility of telling the children they were dating. He knew Lucy already suspected, and judging by her approving nods when he visited, he was hopeful she'd be pleased. Will hung on his every word, though he wanted to tread carefully there. But they'd accepted him, as had Fleur's parents, and her church friends. He was building a life.

And now it was going to be ripped away from him once again.

He couldn't refuse, he knew that. Even if he announced he was leaving the army for good, it was a slow process. He would still have to do the tour. The only way to get out of this without being labelled as AWOL would be to claim medical incompetency. And that would mean admitting his mental health was suffering. Could he do that?

It was just six months. Then he could leave. He could announce his intentions before he left on tour, and then when it ended, he'd be free.

But free for what? His only experience was the army. And what if Fleur wouldn't wait? She'd waited for Jeff, but he hadn't come home.

And that was the real fear. *What if he never came back?*

He realised Jarrop was talking, filling him in on some of the details, and he tried to drag his attention back to the present, but the news whirled through his mind.

He had a week, and he'd have to say goodbye to Fleur. He felt like screaming at the unfairness of it all. This couldn't be right.

This couldn't be God's plan for him, surely?

As Jarrop finally dismissed him, Callum managed to retain his composure until he was out of the man's sight, then he practically broke into a run.

He needed to see the chaplain.

John was poring over a book when Callum burst into his office without knocking. He looked up with a frown, but his expression quickly changed to one of concern. "Has something happened?"

Callum nodded, raking his hand through his hair, barely able to get his words out. "I've been recalled to active service. Iraq. Six months." And once he was out there, Callum knew that six months could easily turn into longer. He closed his eyes and grimaced.

"Sit down," John said as he cleared his desk.

Callum inhaled deeply and sat opposite the chaplain who had become his friend. He looked down at his hands—they were visibly shaking.

"This has clearly hit you hard."

Callum folded one arm and held his cheek with the other and tried to calm himself. "It was a complete shock. I...I can't leave Fleur. Not for six months."

"I can imagine that. I know how happy she's made you."

But John knew that wasn't the only reason, and the chaplain sat patiently, waiting for Callum to talk.

"I can't go," he whispered eventually. "I can't go back." He flinched as scenes of carnage from his last tour flashed through his mind. "It's not about me," he said, his voice stronger now. "I feel I've got more to live for now, but it's not about my life. I can't watch more men die. And," he swallowed hard, "I won't kill. I can't. Not now."

John nodded. "Then tell them that. You could conscientiously object. On religious grounds."

Callum hadn't thought of that. It was an option he was only vaguely aware existed. It made sense. He was a Christian now. How could he go to war and kill, even if it was in defence? He knew it was more complicated than that, but right now, he doubted he could aim a rifle at another human being and shoot to kill. Then he heard his father's voice in his head. He knew what his father thought of those who refused to fight.

Coward.

He shook his head. "I can't do that."

"There's the PTSD. You never took my advice to talk to anyone about it. It's not too late."

But it was. Callum knew it. If he saw someone now, it'd be seen as a last-ditch effort to shirk his responsibilities, especially now that his nightmares had stopped. He had no choice. He'd have to go, and he told John that.

John reached for his Bible, flicked through it, and finding the passage he wanted, passed it to Callum. "Read this," he said quietly. Callum looked down at the page. Joshua chapter one, verse nine. He read, hesitantly, as this was a part of the Bible he wasn't yet familiar with.

"Be strong and courageous; do not be frightened or dismayed, for the Lord your God is with you wherever you go." Callum let out a long sigh. "I still don't understand why God would want me to go. Not now." He passed the Bible back to John.

"We don't always know or understand what God has set in front of us, or why we go through sudden hardship, but there's always a purpose. Keep your eyes fixed on God, Callum. He'll be with you and He'll guide you, and He can teach you through this."

Callum nodded slowly. He knew he had no choice. And once this final tour was over, he could leave for good. Maybe this is what he needed to do, to wrestle with his demons once and for all.

But he still had to tell Fleur.

CHAPTER 10

*C*allum kissed Fleur on the cheek before she slid into the passenger seat of his car. She looked as beautiful as ever in cotton trousers and a loose top that fell from one shoulder. Her hair was pinned up in a messy bun and loose tendrils trailed down her neck. "You look lovely," he said, gazing at her tenderly.

She smiled. "Thank you. I must have changed three times. I feel really nervous."

"There's no need—my parents will love you." He knew he was right. His mother would be delighted with Fleur, and his father would certainly approve of him marrying a seasoned army wife if it went that far, which he was already hoping it would. It was him who was nervous. He loved his parents, but as he'd grown older and come into maturity as a man, he saw eye to eye with his overbearing father less and less.

He knew, too, that his father would be pleased he'd been called back to active service and would no doubt be hoping

Callum would give up his teaching job and return to the field for good.

Part of Callum knew that when he finally told his father he was leaving permanently, regardless of his father's reaction, there'd be a sense of relief in finally getting his decision out into the open. He wouldn't be telling him today though. Today was about them meeting Fleur.

He hadn't told Fleur yet. He had to, but he hadn't wanted to ruin the day. Not just that. He was scared she'd call off their relationship. That he'd lose her as soon as he'd found her. Already the thought of possibly losing her was unbearable. Even so, he knew he had to tell her soon, with less than a week before he left. It was only a six-month tour, he kept telling himself, then remembered that he and Fleur had known each other for less than three. Six months was a long time. Long enough for everything to change.

"Is everything okay?" she asked, concern lacing her voice. "You seem really quiet."

Callum bit his lip and put on a bright face. "Just a little nervous about seeing my parents. My dad always manages to put me on edge." Well, he wasn't lying at least. "But I'm certain they're going to adore you."

"Are you worried your dad is going to go on about you leaving active service?" Fleur asked, obviously remembering their earlier conversations. Callum flinched but tried to keep his thoughts from showing on his face. It certainly wasn't the right time to tell her now, when she was anxious about meeting his family.

"He's complained enough on the phone," he replied, "but

I'm sure he won't miss the opportunity to continue the discussion face to face."

Fleur smiled at him sympathetically. "I bet he's really proud of you deep down."

Callum thought about that. It was true on one level; his father was proud of his medals and his achievements, but that wasn't quite the same thing as being proud of his son for his own sake. Somehow though, it mattered less and less now that he'd given his life to God and felt secure in his Heavenly Father's unconditional love. His dad was, after all, only human. His new faith was helping Callum forgive any grievances he still held, though it was a work in progress.

It was a long, three-hour drive, and Callum was reluctant to talk much so as not to betray the fact that there was more going on inside him than his words let on. He turned the radio to a soft rock channel as he drove. Thankfully, Fleur seemed happy enough, singing along and watching out the window as the scenery passed by. It was rare for her to do anything without the children on weekends. They were with Amy and Angus, and he guessed she was enjoying the break. He sneaked a glance at her. She was singing away without embarrassment, the wind pulling tendrils out of her bun and dancing them around her face. She was so exquisite his heart ached.

Lord, don't let me lose her, he prayed. He tried to recall the scripture that John had given him and hoped he'd have enough faith to trust God to get him through this season and bring him back home safely to her, because the thought of losing her now filled him with despair.

After a while, she closed her eyes and rested her head against the window. He turned the radio off and continued driving in silence with his window down, enjoying the wind rushing through his hair. For the next six months, it would be desert wind, hot and unrelenting. He tried to ignore the foreboding in the pit of his stomach and the nausea that came over him when he thought of being back in that hellhole. It was too much. He sucked in the cool air and tried to concentrate on the day ahead.

They pulled up outside his parents' home, an old, sturdy brick house sitting high on a ridge overlooking Port Phillip Bay. His parents had moved there when his father retired five years earlier. Callum gently nudged Fleur awake.

She sat with a start. "I can't believe I fell asleep!" she exclaimed as she started to fuss with her hair in the mirror and reapply her lipstick.

"You look perfect," he told her, and he meant it. He took her arm as they walked up the drive.

His mum must have been waiting at the window because she opened the door before he had a chance to knock. She pulled him into a warm embrace, kissing him on both cheeks, before turning to Fleur.

"You must be Fleur. How lovely to meet you," she said with sincerity.

Fleur smiled back. "Nice to meet you, too, Mrs. Westaway."

"Oh, please call me Marjorie. Come in. You must be tired."

She ushered them inside and Callum felt the familiar tightening in his chest. Even before he saw his father, he'd squared his shoulders and stiffened, his military bearing even more exaggerated than usual.

His dad was standing by the French windows looking over the garden and the bay, pipe in hand. He nodded to Callum as he and Fleur entered, then his eyes quickly turned to Fleur, appraising her. Callum felt the same as always when seeing his father after having been away for some time. Like a little boy desperate to earn his approval, mixed with a surly teenager who didn't quite have the courage to rebel. Callum had spent his whole adult life being told he was brave, but around his father he felt anything but.

"Good to see you, lad," his father said. The older man smiled thinly at Fleur. "So, you're the young lady who's finally captured our son's heart after all these years." He held out a hand to Fleur, who shook it, looking for all the world like she was about to curtsey. His overbearing father had that effect on people.

"Come into the kitchen, dear, while I make coffee." His mother motioned to Fleur to go with her.

Fleur glanced in Callum's direction and they shared a smile before she followed his mother, leaving Callum alone with his father.

The man continued to look out over the garden as he spoke. "Seems like a nice girl."

"She is."

"Are you going to marry her?" His father put his pipe in his mouth and turned to face Callum, looking him up and down.

Callum blinked. He hadn't been expecting that. Part of him wanted to tell his father it was none of his business, but instead, he replied, "It's early days, Dad, but maybe." Until now, the thought of marrying Fleur had been an abstract idea, something to consider down the track, but having his father ask so bluntly, and with the call-up hanging heavily over his head like a dark cloud, the idea of marrying Fleur suddenly seemed less abstract.

Maybe he should propose before he went on tour. If she accepted, which he sensed she would, it would be bittersweet to then be separated for six months, but it would give them both time to think and reflect, and something to look forward to.

"You're not getting any younger, son. I wouldn't be wasting too much time if I were you."

Callum's lips thinned with irritation as his father turned to the window again, smoke billowing from the corner of his mouth. His father certainly knew how to ruffle him. "Thanks, Dad, but I don't know that age has anything to do with it."

His father shrugged. "Suit yourself. Thought you might be ready to settle down."

Callum scratched the back of his head, his forehead creasing. It was an unusual sentiment from his father. Usually they talked about Callum's most recent deployments and where he might be sent next, or his father would reminisce over his highly decorated past. They rarely spoke of Callum's personal life. However, the man was right. He was ready to settle down. More than ready. If only he hadn't been called up.

His mother returned with a tray containing a pot of coffee and a plate of freshly baked scones which she set down on the large coffee table between two matching couches. Fleur followed her in and immediately looked at him, her brow slightly raised as if to ask how he was doing.

As their gazes connected, a small smile lifted the corner of his mouth. Thoughts of proposing to her floated around in his head. He'd known there was something special about her from the very beginning, but now his heart swelled with feelings he'd never expected to experience again. He loved her. He loved everything about her. Her poise, her depth of character, her love for God and all mankind. She was a brilliant mother, and no doubt, would be a brilliant wife. He held her gaze for a moment, barely daring to dream that he could ask her before he left on tour. But then his mother spoke, inviting them all to sit. "Don't let the coffee go cold."

Callum tore his gaze away and offered to pour the coffee for everyone before sitting beside Fleur. She and his mother seemed to have a lot to talk about. Fleur was interested in the house and its history, and his mother was more than happy to share what she knew about it. It was a lovely home, and he knew how much she liked living there after residing in army housing for the entirety of his father's career.

The day passed pleasantly enough, and as the afternoon wore on, Callum found himself relaxing. His mother clearly adored Fleur and his father, too, seemed impressed and was on his best behaviour, refraining from interrogating her like a drill sergeant, one of the scenarios he'd been worried about. Callum studied Fleur as she ate and talked, and love for her overwhelmed him. His heart ached at the thought of being separated from her.

Her brow creased when she glanced at him while they were sitting on the deck drinking tea. He quickly shoved his thoughts away and smiled, but sensed she'd seen something in his expression that puzzled, and possibly concerned her.

Later, as they drove home, an awkward silence grew between them as his sleek i30 ate up the miles. It was hard to talk when all he could think about was his call-up and how to break the news to her, and whether he should propose before he left on tour.

At last, Fleur turned to him and asked, "What's wrong, Callum? I thought it went quite well with your parents. Did I do something wrong?"

He winced. "Not at all. They adored you." He released a heavy sigh and swallowed hard. He had to tell her. There was no way to put it off any longer. Pulling into a layby, he turned off the engine and stared out the window without seeing.

Fleur laid a hand on his arm. "What is it, Callum?"

He closed his eyes and answered without looking at her. "I've been called up. A six-month active tour of duty in Iraq."

Silence. He didn't dare look at her, but when she removed her hand from his arm, his heart sank.

"You can't refuse?"

Feeling wretched, he slowly turned to face her and shook his head. She looked crestfallen. "Not unless I go AWOL. I could try conscientiously objecting, but it's a long process and I'm not sure I'd be doing it for the right reasons." He inhaled deeply. "I've always known this could happen, but I certainly didn't expect it to be so soon, if ever."

"How long have you known?"

He grimaced. "A few days."

He heard her sharp intake of breath. "Seriously? And you didn't tell me?"

"I didn't know how. I'm sorry. I've barely processed it myself. I haven't told my parents either. I just wanted to get the visit out of the way. Honestly Fleur, I didn't plan on telling you like this."

"So, how did you plan it?"

He shrugged and shook his head. "I guess I would have told you tonight."

"I don't know what to say. It's not your fault you've been called up, but you should have told me as soon as you learned of it." The look of hurt in her eyes ripped at his heart.

He reached out to her. "I'm so sorry, Fleur. Please forgive me."

She studied him for a moment and he wondered what was going through her mind. She took a deep breath and met his gaze. The love and compassion he saw in her eyes blew him away. "This can't be easy for you. Of course I'll forgive you."

Tears stung his eyes. He brushed them away. "Thank you."

"So, how are you doing? Really?"

"Not great," he said honestly, while pinching the bridge of his nose. "I've tried to accept that it's happening, but truly, I don't want to go. John says that God will use this call-up for His purposes and will bring good out of it, but I'm struggling to accept that."

She rubbed his arm. "I'm sure he's right. God can use anything for His glory."

Callum nodded. He knew that, but right now it didn't make him feel any better about the impending separation. "Where does this leave us, Fleur?"

She didn't answer, though her eyes brimmed with tears. He hated the anguish he was putting her through.

He reached out and took her hand, rubbing her skin with his thumb as he gazed into her eyes. "Six months is a long time, but I was hoping you'd wait. I want us to have a future."

"So do I," she said softly, "but will it really be six months?

Jeff used to go on tours that were only supposed to last so long and he'd be gone a year or more."

Callum knew she was right. There were never any guarantees once you were out in the field. There was no guarantee you would even come home.

His grip on her hands tightened, and before he could stop himself, he blurted out, "Fleur, marry me."

Her head jolted up and her eyes widened. "Marry you?"

"Yes. I want us to be together for the rest of our lives. And as my wife to be, you'll get more support while I'm away."

She grew still and expressionless. When she spoke, it was as though her voice came from somewhere far away. "I never thought much of the support from the army when I was Jeff's wife. I don't think a hasty wedding is the answer to this." She pulled her hand from his.

He felt the sting of rejection and the awful, gut-wrenching realisation that in attempting to keep her close, he'd pushed her away. "Fleur," he began, almost pleading, but she cut him off.

"I can't, Callum. Please don't ask me again. When... No. *If* you come back, that's the time to talk about us having a future."

He felt crushed. She turned away and stared out the window. He revved the engine and pulled back out onto the main road, sending gravel flying, his head and heart whirling.

They drove back in silence. He took her to Amy's place and held the door open for her. He'd hoped to spend more time with her and the children, but that wasn't going to happen.

"I'll phone you," she said, kissing his cheek dutifully before walking up Amy's drive. She didn't look back. He watched her go and felt the nauseating sinking of despair before he slowly climbed back in his car and drove home.

He sat outside his house for a long while, reluctant to go inside, as if going inside would make it real, somehow. She'd said no. He'd asked her to marry him, and she'd said no.

He shook his head at his own stupidity. Of course she had. He'd just hit her with bad news, news that must surely have brought back memories of losing Jeff, and in practically the same breath, he'd asked her to be his wife. He hadn't told her any of the things he felt. How much he loved her and how much he wanted to spend his life with her. He'd made his proposal sound more like a practical proposition. *Did he really expect her to say yes?*

He laid his head on the steering wheel, overcome with despair and prayed, *Lord, if it's Your will, let us find a way to work this out and be together. Let this not be the end.*

With a heavy sigh he exited his car, feeling bleak at the prospect of a lonely evening ahead. This would be life on Civvy Street without Fleur, he realised. He couldn't think of anything worse. In fact, he'd rather spend the rest of his life on tour than attempt to live a normal life without her. She was his world, and it had taken the prospect of losing her to truly understand how much she meant to him. She was his soulmate, fashioned for him like he was fashioned for her. The Sarah to his Abraham, the Ruth to his Boaz, the Sheba to his Solomon.

And he'd blown it.

CHAPTER 11

*L*ater that night, when the children were in bed, Fleur wept in Amy's arms. Amy stroked her hair, making soothing sounds in an attempt to comfort her. Fleur hadn't cried like this since Jeff died. The news of Callum's call-up had revived so many memories, but more than that, a gamut of conflicting emotions swamped her, tearing her apart.

After some time, when she'd wept so much there were no more tears left, she wiped her eyes, straightened slowly, looked at Amy and whispered, "I'm sorry."

Amy tutted. "For what? I'm your friend. Tears can be healing, Fleur. You and I both know that."

"I know. I just don't understand why I'm so upset. I've only known him a few months and the tour is only six months. It shouldn't feel like such a big deal."

"You feel how you feel," Amy said. "There is no right or wrong."

Her friend was right. Suppressing her feelings—as she'd done in the car when Callum had told her—only distanced her from him and from God. Yet in that moment, denial had been easier than trying to absorb and process the depth of her pain.

"What I don't understand," she said hesitantly, trying to articulate the deep grief she felt, "is why this feels so much like when Jeff died. That's so out of proportion isn't it? Do you think it's just triggering old feelings?"

"Maybe," Amy said thoughtfully. "I'm sure that's part of it. But have you considered that it isn't so much old feelings as the same feeling, revisited in a different scenario?"

Fleur frowned at her friend. "That sounds like psychobabble. What do you mean?"

"Well," Amy said patiently, "what's the fear?"

"I don't get it."

"Right now, in this moment, in this situation, what are you most afraid of?"

"I don't know," Fleur said, but even as she spoke the words, she knew that wasn't quite true. She *did* feel fear. *Dear God, help me*, she prayed. *Help me face what I need to face.* There was a moment of clarification, when the very air around her seemed to stop moving and the truth hit like a punch to the gut. Her eyes filled with tears again.

"I love him," she gasped to Amy, who reached out and held her hands. "I love him, and I'm terrified I'm going to lose him the same way I lost Jeff and I won't be able to cope. I'm afraid I'll fall apart. I can't do it again, Amy."

Amy embraced her. "I know," she said soothingly. "Of course you feel like this. It's perfectly natural."

"You're going to tell me to give it to God aren't you?" Fleur said, smiling through her tears.

Amy gave a chuckle. "Well, that was kind of what I was going to say, I guess. Who else can lead you through the valley of the shadow of death if not our Lord?"

Fleur nodded. That psalm had always comforted her, and she knew through hard-won experience that it was true. "It just feels so unfair."

"It does seem unfair. Horribly unfair. But we don't know the bigger picture yet, do we? After he does this tour, won't he be able to leave for good?"

"I'm not sure. I didn't ask him, and I don't know if completely cutting ties with the military is even what he wants. But I know one thing," she said resolutely, feeling a new sense of courage fill her, "I will not be an army wife again."

"Then you need to tell him that."

"But I can't tell him what to do!"

"You won't be. You'll simply be telling him what you will not accept. Fleur, I'm going to say something I wanted to say to you a long time ago but never did because Jeff died, and it was not appropriate. You were *never* happy as an army wife. You lived on tenterhooks the whole time, and you were lonely."

A sob ripped through Fleur. Amy was right. It sounded awful to admit to herself now, but there were many nights when she'd lain awake at night, praying that Jeff would choose another path so they could be a regular family. Then he'd died, and she'd pushed those memories away, unable to bear the guilt they caused her.

"I feel almost like I caused Jeff's death," she whispered now, giving voice to a demon she'd carried around with her for so long that it had been buried deep in her subconscious. "I prayed for him to leave the army even though he loved it. I wasn't supportive like a wife should be. And he was taken from me. I feel like I'm being punished now."

Amy squeezed her hands. "No," she said decisively, "that's not true, Fleur. I bet every army wife feels like that from time to time. Jeff's death was not your fault. And our God is a God of love. There is *no* condemnation in Christ. Callum hasn't come into your life as a punishment; this is a blessing. Maybe we can't see how or why right now, but I feel that down to the depth of my soul."

A wave of gratitude flowed through Fleur for her friend, and she also realised that after her heart-wrenching confession, she felt lighter and freer. "Will you pray for me?"

Amy smiled. "Of course I will." Taking Fleur's hands in hers, she bowed her head and began. "Heavenly Father, comfort Fleur in her hour of need. Help her know that You are always with her, even in the depths of despair, even in the valley. *Especially* in the valley. Hold her with Your love in these moments, and in line with Your will, show her what path to take. Fill her heart with Your blessings, Lord, and take the burden of guilt and shame from her so that she may remember who she truly is. Your much-loved daughter."

Peace flooded Fleur's heart, and her resolve and courage welled up and grew firmer. She knew God's presence in her life would sustain her, and He would never leave her or forsake her. "Thank you," she said to her friend.

Amy smiled and let go of her hands. "You're more than welcome."

They sat quietly for a few moments, then Fleur asked, "So, do I wait for him?"

"What does your heart say?"

"That I love him." The truth of those words rang deeply in her soul. "And that's worth waiting for. But this has to be the one and only time. It's not just me who would suffer. The children can't go through another loss."

Amy nodded. "Then tell him that. He must be going out of his mind, wondering what you're thinking."

"Not just that," Fleur said carefully, not wanting to reveal too much of Callum's private feelings, "but I know he's struggling with his experiences in the field. This must feel like being re-traumatised all over again."

"Then we should pray for him, too. This can't be an easy burden for him to bear."

"You're right, and the last thing he needs is me making it harder."

"Maybe not, but what you want is important too, Fleur," Amy reminded her. "Just be honest with him. Tell him what you need so that he'll have enough knowledge to make his decisions."

Fleur nodded. She'd phone him in the morning and arrange to spend some proper time with him before he left. She couldn't let him leave not knowing how she felt.

"And what about the proposal?" Amy asked. "In the middle of all this, there's the fact he asked you to marry him!'

A smile trembled over Fleur's lips. Thinking about it that way, joy began to creep back in. Callum wanted to marry her… "I think he only asked me because of the call-up."

"You don't know that. And if the call-up made him examine how he really feels, is that such a bad thing?"

"I suppose not." Fleur let out a small chuckle. "It's probably a good thing."

"I think it is."

"Would you like another drink?" Fleur asked.

"I think I should call it a night, but thanks anyway." Amy stood and gathered her belongings.

Fleur walked her to the door and hugged her. "Thank you. I honestly don't know what I'd do without you."

"Nor me you," Amy said, returning her hug.

Fleur waved as her friend walked down the path to her car. After Amy drove off, Fleur closed the door and glanced at the phone on the hallway stand. Was it too late to call Callum rather than leave them both to get through the night wondering? With a deep breath, she dialled his number.

He answered after two rings. "Fleur?"

"Callum."

She heard him breathe a sigh that sounded like relief. "I'm so glad you called. I should never have blurted things out like I did. I'm so sorry."

"It's alright. I understand. I wanted to ask if we could see each other before you go so we can talk things through." She swallowed the lump in her throat. "I don't want to lose you, Callum."

His voice grew soft. "I don't want to lose you, either, Fleur."

She rigidly held her tears in check as they arranged to see each other in a few days' time, the night before he left. It barely gave them any time together, but he had a list a mile long to attend to, and it was the only time he had to spare. She felt a little deflated, but then told herself that any time together was a blessing.

They wished each other good night and she went to bed feeling lighter. She didn't know what the future held, but she knew who held it, and that God would be right there beside her.

CHAPTER 12

*C*allum watched the clock while waiting for Fleur. The hands moved torturously slowly, yet at the same time, he almost didn't want the time of her arrival to come.

The sooner she came, the sooner he'd have to say goodbye to her for the next six months. Although her phone call had given him hope that this didn't have to be the end of their relationship, leaving her for any length of time was crushing.

He didn't want to admit it to himself, but he was also terrified of what he was leaving her for. He'd never felt this way before a tour; he'd always welcomed the challenge and been more focused on his men than himself. The goal was to achieve the objective and get the job done with as few casualties as possible. Now he had no idea how it would feel to be back in the field. He wasn't scared of being hurt, but of seeing others hurt and once again being able to do nothing about it. The 'enemy' was on his mind this time as well. While those soldiers may be on the 'opposite side' and certainly a danger, they were

God's children, too. The futility of it all loomed before him, large in his consciousness.

God help me. Help us all. As John had been reminding him all week, there were no easy answers, but he needed to trust God to lead him.

Sometimes it was more about figuring out the right questions. Callum had spent every spare moment while at work with John or reading scripture and had found some comfort in the Psalms. Reading how the prophets of old had wrestled with questions of war and peace, enmity and love, had given him some insight and hope. As wretched as he felt, he knew that without his newfound faith, it would be a lot worse.

The nightmares hadn't returned. Although he was too anxious to sleep well and had expected a resurgence of his night terrors, none had come. The Lord was walking with him through this already.

The last few days had been highly emotional in every way. Even Jarrop was sad at his impending departure, and the recruits looked devastated, particularly Billy, who was still waiting to hear about his application to be a medic. Callum was praying for him every day, too. He was going to miss them. Even if he returned to Salford to work out his notice after the tour, which was the most logical option, this particular bunch of recruits would have moved on to Trade Training and he would have a whole new cohort. He had really wanted to be around for their marching out parade.

He was going to miss Lucy and Will, too. Fleur had phoned him the previous evening for him to say goodbye to them on the phone. He'd kept his explanation light, not giving the details of where he'd been sent and promising to take them to the beach when he returned, but he'd heard both the resignation in Lucy's voice and the fear in Will's.

They thought he wasn't coming back.

In just a few short months, the children had touched his heart so much that he knew he was almost as attached to them as he was to Fleur. While he would never try—or want—to replace Jeff as their father, he'd hoped to be a good role model for them.

And you will be, he told himself firmly. *You're going to come back, and everything is going to be fine.*

The doorbell rang and Callum jumped up, taking a few deep breaths before opening the door.

"Fleur." As overwhelming love filled him, it was all he could do not to gather her in his arms and kiss her. As their gazes met and held, she stepped slowly into his embrace and he buried his face in her hair, inhaling her sweet smell.

She pulled back and when she looked at him, he saw both sorrow and longing in her eyes. Without realising what he was about to do, his lips were suddenly on hers and he kissed her with a passion that had been building all week.

She responded with an urgency that both surprised and delighted him. Having her in his arms felt so right and long overdue, as if she should have been there all along. She pressed her body into his, her hands in his hair, and Callum felt himself getting swept up in the moment, drinking in the sensations.

He had to muster every ounce of self-control to break the kiss and step back. He took her hands in his and gazed into her eyes. "Wow," he said, unable to formulate a rational response.

She smiled shyly. With her hair mussed, she looked irresistible. "I'm sorry," she said breathlessly, although she didn't look sorry at all. "I'm going to miss you so much."

"Not as much as I'm going to miss you." He led her into the lounge room and they sat down together, still holding hands. She curled her legs beneath her and leaned on him. They sat that way for a few moments, enjoying each other's presence in the bittersweet knowledge of their looming separation.

"What time do you fly out?" she asked eventually.

"Seven hundred...sorry, seven am."

She laughed. "It's alright, I got used to speaking in military time with Jeff."

At the mention of Jeff they both fell silent again, lost in their thoughts. Straightening so he could look at her, Callum spoke first. "I know this must be hard for you, Fleur, particularly after your experience with Jeff. I'm so glad you haven't called it off between us, but I would have understood if you had."

She nodded slowly. "I thought about it, but I haven't come this far and allowed myself to love again just to run away at the first hurdle. God will give me strength. But you're right—it is hard. Thank God for Amy. She's really helped me."

He was glad she had a friend like Amy, although it highlighted how lonely his past few years had been. He'd lost too many friends in war to now find it easy to make them. "She's a lovely woman. I'm glad she'll be here for you while I'm gone."

"What about you? This isn't just about our relationship. How are you feeling about going back?"

Callum winced. Fleur had a knack of always getting right to the emotional heart of the matter. "Scared," he admitted. "Not so much of something happening to me, but just of being back out there, back in the thick of it all. I don't even know if I've got it in me anymore. I've changed."

He said the last with a pang of shame, and hearing it, Fleur put her palm to his cheek. "That's not a bad thing, Callum. Don't be ashamed of becoming a better person. You've changed because you've given yourself to the Lord and He's opened your heart. I know it doesn't always feel like the best thing when we're going through it, but challenges lead to growth, if we let them."

At the conviction in her voice, Callum knew she spoke not just from knowledge of scripture but from her own personal experiences, and he loved her for both her openness and her strength.

"You're a special woman, Fleur," he said, while tracing his finger along her hairline and gazing into her eyes.

"Don't you forget it." She grinned and laid her head on his chest.

He kissed the top of her head. If only they could stay like this forever and the morning would never come.

"I love you," he muttered into her hair, and as he said it, he knew it was true. He'd never loved like this before, never with this strength of devotion and the certainty they were made for each other. Fashioned for one another.

Fleur stilled in his arms. He held his breath as he waited for her response. Had he said too much too soon again?

She looked up at him with tears glistening in her eyes. "I love you, too," she whispered.

Feeling as though his heart would burst with joy, he breathed a sigh of relief. "Thank goodness," he said with a half-laugh. "I thought my proposal had scared you right off."

She let out a small chuckle and then grew serious. "If I didn't feel that way about you, I would *never* put myself through this again. Waiting for you while you're on tour, I mean. You've captured my heart, Callum Westaway, and I'll wait for you this once, but I can't do it again after that. I'm sorry. I hope you understand."

"Absolutely." He smoothed some wisps of hair off her face as he gazed into her eyes. "This is my last tour, of that I'm sure." He pulled her close and hugged her.

"I'm glad to hear that." She leaned against him and then said, "About that ill-timed proposal of yours..."

Callum felt himself flush. "I'm so sorry." He drew a long breath, and placing his finger under her chin, tipped her head so he could look into her eyes. "I do want that, but it wasn't the right time nor was it done the right way."

She glanced down, clasping her hands as if nervous before looking back up. "Well, I just wanted you to know...if you were to ask me again when you get back, the answer will be yes."

Callum closed his eyes, squeezing back tears as he silently uttered a prayer of thanks. When he opened them again, Fleur's eyes were glistening. He smiled, all his worries momentarily slipping away. "I'm so glad," he said quietly, pulling her close once more and kissing the side of her head as he wrapped his arms around her. She felt so good, and he didn't want the moment to end. It seemed she didn't, either, as she leaned against his chest, stroking his arm. Neither wanted to break the silence nor address their imminent separation.

Finally, she stirred. She'd grown so still, he'd wondered if she'd fallen asleep. "I guess it's time to go," she said, straightening. Although she smiled, sorrow had returned to her eyes.

"I wish you didn't have to." He stood and helped her to her feet and walked her to the door.

She paused in the doorway, looking up at him now with unabashed tears. "Stay safe, Callum." Her voice broke on a half-smothered sob. His own tears threatening, he gathered her into his arms.

They kissed again, a long, lingering goodbye kiss that neither wanted to end. She finally broke away, and gazing into his eyes, squeezed his hand before walking to her car. She blew him a kiss as she got in and brushed her eyes as she drove away.

He looked down the street for a long time after she'd driven out of sight, sending silent prayers after her.

Only as he shut the door did he realise tears were streaming down his own face, too.

CHAPTER 13

FIVE WEEKS LATER

*L*t Cl Westaway looked intently at the dust road ahead of him as he steered the jeep. Three of his men sat in the back, primed and ready for any ambush. They were delivering much needed supplies to the next outpost, but this road was known to be both treacherous and often booby trapped with homemade explosives.

He'd been on tour for a month, and already his life back home—because Salford was home now, thanks to Fleur—seemed eons away. It was amazing how quickly he'd slipped back into a military role. He seemed to function on auto pilot. After being away from the field and confronting so many demon, the fears that he would be unable to fulfil his duties had been unfounded.

He wasn't entirely sure that was a good thing, however. He

seemed to be existing in a place of slight disassociation, removed from what was going on around him and emotionally detached. He wondered if it hadn't always been this way. It was just that he was more self-aware and able to notice it now.

Either way, he still couldn't wait to get home. *One month down, five to go.* So far, the tour had been reasonably uneventful, if not, in fact, boring. Days and days at the outpost, scanning the horizon, with nothing happening. Not that he wanted anything to happen. When he'd been a green recruit, he'd almost craved the excitement, anything to break the monotony. A few years and the loss of good men later, and the reality had relieved him of that particular naiveté.

He missed Fleur. In fact, every evening when he turned in, she was on his mind. She haunted his dreams and was his first thought when he woke in the morning. Not being able to speak to her was driving him crazy. He'd expected some form of communication, but they'd been literally stationed in the middle of nowhere. He'd written her a letter nearly every day, but there was no way of mailing them to her. He hoped he wouldn't have to go the whole six months without any contact whatsoever.

As he turned a corner, he felt a familiar sense of unease in his gut. Something was wrong. He slowed the jeep and sent up a quick prayer.

"Sir?" asked one of his men. "Is everything okay?"

"Yes. Just being cautious." Yet his every instinct screamed danger.

There was a sudden pull on his arm and he sharply turned the wheel, sending the jeep to the side of the road. He faced a moment of confusion, because although it was him who'd made the movement, it was as though a force outside himself had compelled him to do it. He opened his mouth to shout a warning to his men, but his voice was lost in the sound of an explosion. Searing pain ripped through one side of his body, and his last conscious thought was that his nightmare was going to come true and he would never see Fleur again. A sudden image of her face flashed before him, her beautiful eyes, staring at him as though she was directly in front of him. Her lips were moving but he couldn't make out what she was saying.

Then everything went black.

FLEUR WAS DISTRACTED as she drove the children to school, as much as she tried to focus on the day ahead.

She hadn't heard a word from Callum in nearly six weeks, and while she knew there might be no correspondence because of where he was, she couldn't chase away the feeling that something terrible had happened to him. The feeling just wouldn't leave her.

She dropped Will and Lucy off and made her way to work, doing her best to get through CrossFit and Pilates, but her panic was growing. Something was happening, she was sure of it. As she worked, she sent up silent prayers for Callum.

Later, driving home after work, she thought about the laundry she needed to do before the next school run. Her days had settled into the same comforting yet boring rhythm they had been before she'd met Callum, but now without him, a big part of her life just felt empty. She missed him so much it hurt.

She was loading the washing machine when the phone rang. She sprinted for it, her breath catching in her throat.

"Fleur?"

"Callum?" she gasped. But even as she spoke his name, she knew she was wrong.

"I'm afraid not. This is his father, and I've got bad news."

CALLUM OPENED his eyes to find himself walking across a field of wildflowers. It was a place that seemed familiar, and yet at the same time, he knew he'd never been there before. The air was fresh with the scent of those flowers, and he felt wonderfully at peace. He couldn't remember how he'd gotten there, but he was sure he was supposed to meet someone; he just couldn't remember who.

How odd.

He had a vague memory of a loud noise and a road... He'd been going somewhere, somewhere important. It didn't seem important now.

As he carried on walking, he heard the clear sound of running water. A stream was in the distance. He walked to it and sat down. A butterfly fluttered past him, and upstream otters jumped in and out of the water, delighting in it. He smiled to himself. *Fleur would love it here,* he thought.

He felt rather than heard someone sit next to him and he looked up, surprised. A young, dark haired man in army uniform sat there. As Callum stared, dumbfounded, the man idly stirred his hand in the fresh water. Serenity filled his face.

"Jeff?" Callum asked.

The man smiled. A sense of peace radiated from him that made Callum immediately feel calmer. "Hey, sir, good to see you."

"Where are we?"

Jeff smiled. "Nowhere, really. Call it a dream, since that's the closest you'll come to understanding in this life."

Callum frowned, puzzled. He wasn't used to dreams like this. Everything seemed clearer and sharper than real life. *Or was it real life?* He wasn't sure.

"You're not dead?" Callum asked. Then a horrifying thought occurred to him. "Am I dead?"

"No," Jeff replied, to Callum's relief. "You're...resting. Healing. And not just physically. These waters," he swirled his hand in the stream again, "will restore your soul."

Callum frowned at that, knowing Jeff referred to more than just the stream, but even so, he cupped his hands in the stream and drank of the cleanest and most thirst-quenching water he'd ever tasted. Jeff watched him, smiling.

Callum sat back up and took a deep breath. There was something he had to ask. "Fleur..." he began.

Jeff held up a hand. "You don't need to ask. You have my blessing."

"Thank you." Callum didn't know what else to say.

Jeff stood.

"Where are you going?"

"I can't stay here," he said, not answering Callum's question. "I belong...elsewhere."

Callum shook his head. This was all too confusing. "This isn't heaven?"

Jeff laughed. "No. Heaven is *way* better than this. This

is...inside your head. But still real. It doesn't have to make sense," he added when Callum stared at him blankly.

Jeff placed his hand to his forehead and saluted, then turned and strolled across the field before disappearing into the distance. Callum watched him go, bewildered but also strangely at peace.

A hummingbird passed him, and Callum thought how lovely it was here. He wanted to stay longer, but he knew he had to go back.

To Fleur.

FLEUR PRACTICALLY SPRINTED into the hospital room and shed tears of relief when she saw Callum sitting up in bed. His shoulder was bandaged, and he looked thinner than when she'd last seen him, but he was okay. *He was alive.* "Callum!" she exclaimed breathlessly.

When he looked up, his tired expression transformed into one of joy. "Fleur! I didn't know you were coming."

"I spoke to your parents this morning and drove here right away. Thank God, Callum. I had such an awful feeling when I hadn't heard from you; I thought you were dead." She went to throw her arms around him, but he winced and held her back.

She stopped and apologised. "Your shoulder...it hurts?"

He nodded. "Yep. I'll have to have rehab on it to get full movement back. But I'm lucky. It could have been an arm blown off...or worse."

She gave a silent prayer of gratitude. "Was anyone else hurt?" She knew it would tear him apart if he'd lost any men.

"Only superficially, thank the Lord. The weird thing is, I swerved the jeep in time so that the impact of the explosive was minimal, but it was as if it wasn't my hands. And I don't know how I knew there was any danger."

"God was watching over you," she said simply. She took his hand, her eyes brimming. "I'm so glad you're okay, Callum. I can't wait until you can come home."

"Neither can I. I'm being discharged from active service for good. This shoulder will never be the same again."

Fleur felt guilty at the rush of joy that flowed through her. The last thing she wanted was for him to be injured. Nevertheless, maybe it was a blessing in disguise. "Will you go back to the barracks as a trainer?"

Callum shook his head. "I don't need to. I'm being medically discharged, so I don't need to work out any notice. I'll get a decent pension. But...I don't know what I'll do. I'll go stir crazy doing nothing."

"You enjoyed teaching," she pointed out.

"Yes. But I can't in good conscience train those youngsters to go to war. I don't think it's what God wants me to do." He sighed. "I just wish I knew what He does want for me."

Fleur squeezed his hand. "You'll figure it out. God will show you the way. Right now, you just need to concentrate on getting better."

He looked at her with a gleam in his eyes. "There's one thing I know I'm going to do. It's not quite how I imagined it, but...can you open that drawer and pass me the blue parcel?"

Fleur did as he asked. When her fingers closed round a small cube-shaped gift-wrapped box, she knew instantly what it was.

"I bought it the day before I left. Just in case." He laughed. "Open it."

With shaking fingers, she opened it to reveal a small jewellery box. Snapping it open, she glimpsed a beautiful solitaire diamond ring. Tears sprang to her eyes as she stared at it. "It's beautiful."

"I can't go on one knee right now, but Fleur," he reached for her hands and gazed into her tear-filled eyes, "I love you with all my heart and I never want to be separated from you again. Your love has transformed my life. Will you do me the very greatest honour and become my wife?"

This time, she forgot all about his shoulder and threw herself onto his chest, tears of joy streaming down her face.

"Yes," she whispered. "Of course I will."

LATER, Callum lay back against the pillows, exhausted but ecstatically happy. He hadn't planned on proposing to Fleur until he was home, but the moment had felt instinctively right and he'd seized it. He was glad he had.

He looked up as a soft knock sounded on the door. John poked his head in. "Hey, Callum. It's good to see you."

"And you," Callum replied. "Come in. Take a seat."

The chaplain crossed the floor and sat on the chair by the bed. "How are you doing? I came as soon as I heard."

"I'm fine. No, I'm more than fine." Callum couldn't stop himself from grinning as he told John about the proposal. John congratulated him with genuine happiness, and then said, "I have other news you might wish to know."

"Good news?"

He nodded, his mouth tipping in a pleased grin. "I believe so. Young Billy made it into medic training."

Elation rushed through Callum. "Thank God," he whispered.

"Definitely. I think the boy will go far. Also...have you thought about what you're going to do when you get home?"

Callum shook his head, his elation suddenly replaced with despondency. "No." He blew out a heavy breath. "Not yet."

John's eyes twinkled. Frowning, Callum straightened to hear what his friend was about to say.

"It's your choice of course," his brows twitched, "but an opportunity has come up at Salford for a youth leader for young men. They're a challenging lot—young offenders, ex-gang members. A lot like Billy, really. They need a good role model. The leaders are specifically looking for a man of faith with a military or teaching background..." He let his words hang in the air.

Callum stared at him for a moment, trying to take in what he'd heard. "You think I could do it?"

"I think you'd be perfect. If you want it, I'd say it's pretty much yours for the taking. I'll give you a reference, of course."

Callum grabbed the chaplain's hand. "Thank you," he said, pumping his friend's hand enthusiastically.

John shook his head. "It's God you need to thank."

"You're right." Later on, after John left, Callum bowed his head and did just that.

EPILOGUE

The next few months brought many changes. Callum recovered well and took up his post as youth trainer and absolutely loved the challenge of working with troubled young men and women. He'd also begun talking about training for youth ministry, and Fleur had no doubt that he'd be amazing at it. He'd grown and deepened in his faith so much since his return and was now deeply involved with their church. Watching him flourish and bloom was such a blessing. He'd also been receiving counselling for his PTSD and was well on the way to a full recovery.

As for her, she'd been offered a partnership position at the gym which had completely surprised her, but after some reflection and much prayer, she had, of course, accepted. The blessings had been pouring down on them all.

Now, walking down the aisle on her father's arm, she kept her eyes focused firmly on Callum. Although her heart thumped, she forced herself to breathe slowly and keep her pace slow, but all she wanted to do was run down the aisle and jump into his arms.

She was about to marry Callum!

Even now that the ceremony was taking place, the moment felt surreal. God had blessed her greatly by bringing this man into her life. She loved him to bits and couldn't wait to be his wife. Love shone from his eyes, and she offered him a small, shy smile.

"You look beautiful," he mouthed as she reached him. He looked almost as nervous as she felt. She passed her flower bouquet to Lucy, who took it solemnly before taking her seat. Lucy and Will had walked down the aisle arm in arm, followed by Amy, who was radiant in a soft buttery-yellow, knee-length dress.

As Amy took her place at the front, she winked at Fleur. Fleur smiled at her best friend and then turned back to the man who was about to become her husband and took a deep breath. He looked so handsome in his grey suit that the sight of him took her breath away. She loved him so much she thought her heart would burst.

They joined hands at the request of the pastor, who after introducing himself and saying the initial lines, gave a short sermon on marriage. He read several verses from the Song of Solomon, the book Fleur considered the most linguistically beautiful in Scripture.

"'*Place me like a seal over your heart, like a seal on your arm; for love is as strong as death, its passion unyielding as the grave. It burns like blazing fire, like a mighty flame...Many waters cannot quench love and rivers cannot sweep it away. If one were to give all the wealth of one's house for love, it would be utterly scorned. For my beloved is mine, and I am my beloved's.'"*

Fleur's heart welled with love as she gazed into Callum's eyes and the ancient words of Scripture washed over her, blessing their love and their marriage. Callum squeezed her hands and smiled at her.

The pastor continued with his sermon. "A Christian marriage is one ordained by God Himself, a sacred calling in which both parties are called to cherish and uplift the other. Joined together not just in body and heart, but in soul, entwined like a braid. And like a braid there are not two threads but three; husband, wife and God. For when we put God at the centre of our marriage as we do every other part of our lives, we find our marriage is as strong as a braid, entwined in such a way that it cannot easily fray. With God's blessing, the love between husband and wife is grounded in faith, uplifted by the Spirit, and grows stronger every day.

"That is not to say there are never challenges in a marriage. From the days of Adam and Eve there has been discord between man and woman, and modern life brings with it many discontents. However, a Christian marriage is one of forgiveness, hope and the knowledge that there is a way through every valley, with God at our side.

"Let us love each other then as God loves us, wholly and unconditionally and with a love that is as strong as death and as mighty as a flame. I pray that in the joining together of these two, Callum and Fleur, a love that no river can sweep away is sanctified. May we bow our heads together and pray for Callum and Fleur, and for Lucy and Will, for today they all become a family."

He finished and the congregation bowed their heads in prayer. Fleur closed her eyes and smiled as Callum rubbed her hand with his thumbs.

After a few moments of quiet prayer, the pastor led them in their vows to one another. Callum's voice was strong and clear as he looked into her eyes, giving her the confidence to also speak clearly, although tears of joy welled in her eyes as they pledged themselves to each other. For better or worse, richer or poorer, in sickness and in health, til death they do part. She paused at that, thinking suddenly of Jeff, and as she did so, she felt a quiet blessing descend on her and she knew, in an instant, that Jeff's spirit, too, blessed their marriage.

As the pastor pronounced them man and wife and they exchanged rings, she felt like the happiest woman in the world.

The whole church sang 'Amazing Grace', Callum's favourite hymn, together before they went to the desk to sign the registers. Before they did so, the pastor served them communion in another sign of blessing for their marriage. After the registers were signed, they walked arm in arm down the aisle, laughing as they were showered with confetti.

After the photos had been taken, they adjourned to the church hall for the wedding breakfast. Taking her hand after they were seated, Callum leaned close and whispered into her ear, "You look absolutely divine, Mrs. Westaway."

Fleur exhaled a long sigh of contentment and smiled at him. To think that this man was now her husband gave her joy beyond measure.

The first speech was by her father, who did his best to overcome his usual reticence with public speaking to deliver a beautifully sweet speech.

Then it was Callum's father's turn. Fleur felt Callum tense slightly as his father stood. In the months since Callum had left the army, his relationship with his father had fluctuated. The elder Mr. Westaway had expressed his support through Callum's rehabilitation process, and on Callum's first day in his new role as a youth trainer, had signed the congratulations card himself, something Callum had said was unheard of. 'Mum always signs the cards.' Neither father nor son, however, had had anything other than a perfunctory conversation. Fleur knew that Callum was worried what his father would say, if there'd be any veiled criticism in his speech.

Yet it was the exact opposite. After the round of thanks and the toast to Fleur, Mr. Westaway continued. "I'd like to take the chance to say how very proud of my son I am. Not only has he forged two successful careers, one in the army and one in perhaps his true vocation as a teacher and leader, but I've had the pleasure of watching him transform into a man of integrity and honour. We are so pleased that he's found the lovely Fleur, and again I'd like to raise a toast, to my son and his wife."

As the toast was raised, Fleur looked at Callum. He was staring at his lap and she knew he was trying not to show emotion. This was such a hugely healing moment for him. She reached for his hand and squeezed it.

After the speeches, Callum approached his father and shook his hand before pulling him into an embrace. Fleur's eyes filled again as she watched, and she wondered if she'd ever be able to do anything other than laugh or cry tears of joy again. Her emotions were so heightened that the smallest of things brought her to tears.

Neither were the blessings of the day over. As she stepped

outside into the garden for some fresh air while Callum was mingling, she heard someone behind her and turned to see Amy, who pulled her into a heavily scented hug.

"Well done," Amy said, kissing her cheek.

"Thank you. And thank you for being my maid of honour."

Amy chuckled. "As if I'd let you ask anyone else! But listen —I have something to tell you. I was going to wait because this is your day, but I can't keep this from you for another fortnight."

Fleur studied her friend's face and then gasped. "Amy, you're..."

"Pregnant. Yes." Amy's face broke into the broadest grin Fleur had ever seen.

Fleur shrieked and threw her arms around her friend, tears once again streaming down her cheeks.

"Will you be the godmother?"

"Of course! As if I'd let you ask anyone else."

Amy laughed and they hugged again. Fleur felt giddy with excitement. Even if she prayed an all-night vigil, she knew there weren't enough hours in the day to pour out the praise in her heart to God.

LATER THAT NIGHT, after all the festivities had ended and Callum had whisked Fleur away to a beautiful resort hotel in the High Country for their first night together as a married couple, she lay in her husband's arms, her head on his chest. Their wedding day had been everything she'd dreamed of and more. Candles flickered on the dressing table and rose petals scattered the floor where they'd fallen from the bed.

She felt utterly content as Callum stroked her hair. "I love you, Callum," she murmured as she felt herself drifting off to sleep.

"I love you, Fleur," he replied, kissing the top of her head.

As sleep overtook her, her last thought was a refrain from the Scripture the pastor had read aloud before they took their vows. She fell asleep with a smile on her face and joy in her heart.

'O Lord, my healing God,
I cried out for a miracle and You healed me...
We may weep through the night but at daybreak it will turn into
shouts of ecstatic joy...
He has torn the veil and lifted from me the sad heaviness of
mourning.
He wrapped me in the glory garments of gladness.
How could I be silent when it's time now to praise You?
Now my heart sings out loud, bursting with joy—a bliss inside that
keeps me singing.
I can never thank You enough.'

The End

A NOTE FROM THE AUTHOR

I hope you enjoyed *Because We Loved*. There are at least two more books in the **Transformed by Love Christian Romance Series**, so don't miss them!

Because We Forgave, coming soon, is the story of Samuel Jackson, a disgraced game show host, and his ex-wife, Eloise, and their journey to forgiveness. If you liked *Because We Loved*, I'm sure you'll also like this one.

To make sure you don't miss it, and to be notified of all my new releases, why not join my Readers' list? You'll also receive a free thank-you copy of *Hank and Sarah - A Love Story*, a clean love story with God at the center. https://www.julietteduncan.com/subscribe/

Enjoyed *Because We Loved*? You can make a big difference. Help other people find this book by writing a review and telling them why you liked it. Honest reviews of my books help bring them to the attention of other readers just like yourself, and I'd be very grateful if you could spare just five minutes to leave a review (it can be as short as you like) on the book's Amazon page.

Keep reading for a bonus chapter of *Her Kind-Hearted Billionaire*. I think you'll enjoy it.

Blessings,

Juliette

JULIETTE DUNCAN

Her
Kind-Hearted
Billionaire

BILLIONAIRES WITH HEART
CHRISTIAN ROMANCE SERIES

Chapter 1

Sydney, Australia

Nicholas Barrington sat behind his desk on the forty-fifth floor of the tower bearing his family's name and removed his pre-prepared meal from his lunch bag. Below, Sydney Harbour shimmered in the midday sun and looked spectacular. A small tugboat, looking much like a toy from this height, guided a large cruise ship through the harbour towards the heads, while a number of yachts sliced through the water easily in what Nick assumed was a strong breeze, given the trim of their sails. The problem was, being on the forty-fifth floor, he was removed from reality. The view was sensational, but he felt like a spectator. He'd much rather be a participant.

A firm knock sounded on his office door, pulling his gaze from the vista. Nicholas swivelled around. Alden, his brother and fellow director, sauntered in and sank into the chair on the opposite side of the desk. "Taking time for lunch today, bro?" At thirty-one, Alden was two years younger than Nicholas and had the same sea-blue eyes, although his hair was lighter.

"Yes. I was just about to eat. Did you bring yours?" For a moment, Nicholas forgot he was talking with his brother. Of course Alden hadn't brought his lunch.

Alden scoffed, eyeing Nicholas's bag with amusement. "It'll be here in five minutes."

Nicholas pulled out his sandwich and salad, glad he didn't have to wait for his meal to be delivered.

"Eating in here today?" Charity, their younger sister, appeared in the doorway. The sharp bob framing her pixie-like face was the same dark colour as his, but she had their late mother's emerald green eyes. She plopped onto the chair next to Alden and pulled a portable blender filled with green powder from her carry bag. Opening a bottle of water, she poured half of it in and hit the button.

"That looks disgusting," Nicholas shouted over the whir of the machine.

"Try some if you like."

Grimacing, he quickly shook his head. "No thanks. I'll stick to my sandwich."

Moments later, a young man knocked tentatively on the door holding a rectangular food box. Alden waved him in and took the box.

Setting it on the desk, he peeled back the cardboard lid, revealing a large steak with new potatoes and green beans. Although it smelled appetising, as Nicholas took the last bite of his sandwich and moved onto the salad, he was thankful his tastes weren't the same as his siblings. He was a simple man with simple needs.

"It's all right, but it could be better," Alden commented after swallowing his first mouthful.

Nicholas ignored his brother's comment and instead focused on Charity who'd just turned the blender off. The silence was very welcome.

"So, you know I was meant to be flying to Bali tomorrow for that meditation retreat?" Angling her head, she glanced at him as she poured some of the green concoction into a glass.

He nodded. Of late, Charity had been delving into meditation and something about self-praise and how to be her own deity. Not what Nicholas would have considered a worthwhile venture, but, each to his own. He'd started exploring things of a spiritual nature as well, but his initial explorations had led him to a traditional church, although he hadn't yet made up his mind whether that was what he wanted.

"Looks like I'll have to postpone the flight to another day." Charity released a frustrated sigh before taking a mouthful of what Nicholas considered a disgusting looking green concoction.

"Why's that?"

"Why?" Charity's green eyes bulged. "Because of that lazy pilot." Her voice rose to a crescendo and Nicholas wouldn't have been surprised if the whole floor had heard.

"Ugh, don't even get me started." Alden shook his head, waving a fork in the air.

Charity leaned forward. "Can you believe he told me he can't work tomorrow? I mean, I'm his boss. It's not like we're ordering him to fly every day. He gets plenty of time off. I just needed him for one day."

"Why can't he take you?" Nicholas asked in a calm voice.

"His daughter's having surgery. I get that family is important and all that, but honestly, it's only a few hours each way. He'd be back before she even woke up."

Nicholas studied his sister with sadness. He doubted she knew that Roger's small daughter had been born with special needs and her surgeries required extensive preparation. Even the anesthesia was a risk. But it was no use saying anything. She wouldn't understand or care. "Did he suggest anyone else who could step in?"

"I don't want anyone else. They wouldn't know our plane like he does." Charity blew out another breath and sipped her concoction. "Anyway, I think we should fire him." Shifting in her chair, she crossed her long, slim legs and adjusted her skirt.

"I agree," Alden said. "Last time he took me to Dubai, we were an hour late. He said it was because they didn't have a place for us to land, but isn't it his job to make sure all of that's figured out ahead of time?"

Nicholas sighed. "That's hardly his fault. Sometimes unexpected things happen that are out of anyone's control. You know Roger's competent and he always does his best."

"You're so naive, big brother. You always want to see the good in everybody. No wonder they take advantage of you." Alden gave him a withering look.

Nicholas pursed his lips. He wished his siblings could show a little more humility and understanding, especially since they'd been given so much. How could they be so cruel and selfish when it came to others?

Taking a sip from his water bottle, Nicholas shut out his siblings as they continued talking about things he couldn't relate to. Although the three were very different, it saddened him they weren't closer. Without any other family, they only had each other. But all they ever talked about was the business and what gave them pleasure, like Charity's Bali trip. Beyond that, very little of depth ever entered their conversations. While the two continued to talk about things of no interest to him, Nicholas returned to his work, but his ears pricked when Alden mentioned their late grandfather, James Barrington.

"You know, old James wouldn't have liked us wasting the money on a lousy staffer. Just because a man's nice enough doesn't make him worth the money." It seemed they'd returned to the issue of whether to fire Roger or not. Nicholas groaned. From what he remembered of James Barrington, firing a man because of an important family issue would have been the last thing he would have done.

When he died, the three siblings had inherited their grand-father's fortune, amassed during the mining boom of the eighties. A billion for each, plus the company divided between them. Now the trio lacked for nothing, but as much as Nicholas appreciated the life he now had, he would much have preferred his grandfather, and his parents, to still be alive. How different things would have been if his parents had inherited instead of the three grandchildren.

He sighed sadly. Yes, he'd give just about anything to have his parents back. It didn't seem fair that their lives had been snuffed out while they were still in their prime.

"So, do you think we should fire him? After he takes me to Bali, of course?" Charity asked nonchalantly, inspecting her perfectly manicured nails.

"Don't be a fool," Alden said harshly.

For a moment, Nicholas held hopes that his brother might stick up for the man, but they were soon dashed when Alden continued. "You should probably wait until he brings you back from Bali. You don't want to be stuck there!" He laughed, and Charity joined in.

Nicholas seethed. He had to say something, but he needed to remain calm and rational. An emotional defense of the pilot wouldn't go over well with his siblings. "Why don't we give him another chance? His daughter is having surgery, it's hardly a time to be selfish."

Charity huffed with exasperation. "Whatever you say, big brother. Although I don't see how it affects you, since you never use the private jet, anyway." Her voice dripped with sarcasm.

Biting his lip, Nicholas brushed her comments and attitude off. They'd soon forget about the pilot and move on to a discussion about shoes or something as equally trivial.

"Well, I'm headed out. I've got a hot yoga class this afternoon." Charity stood, tossed her rubbish in the bin, and then picked up her blender.

"Don't you need more than that shake before working out?" Alden waved the last piece of steak on his fork as if he were teasing her with it.

She rolled her eyes. "Keep your cow, thanks." With that, she turned and left the room, teetering on her stilettos.

Alden mopped up the last of his gravy, said a brief goodbye to Nicholas, and then also left the office.

Leaning back in his chair, Nicholas released a slow breath and gazed out the window. The cruise ship was long gone, but a Manly ferry was approaching Circular Quay, leaving white frothy water in its wake.

As much as he loved his siblings, he also loved his peace

and quiet. He sometimes wondered about their grandfather and whether he'd be pleased with how his grandchildren were handling his fortune. James Barrington was renowned for his kindness, a rarity in the ruthless mining industry, and Nicholas wished he'd gotten to know him better before he passed. He sensed he could have learned a lot from him, and not just about the business. He'd heard that James Barrington was a religious man. Another rarity in the industry.

Swivelling his chair all the way around, Nicholas set back to work, tapping his fingers on the keyboard, opening emails from clients, studying spreadsheets. Millions of dollars in transactions and exchanges occurred on a weekly basis and the company was doing well, but as Managing Director, he needed to stay on top of it.

Their clients were happy, and he had reason to be proud of the company that he and his siblings had maintained and grown since taking over almost ten years ago. To the world at large, they were a success.

But sometimes, in the still of night, when he had time to think, he pondered what success really was. What was he missing by spending all his days on the forty-fifth floor?

Grab your copy to continue reading *Her Kind-Hearted Billionaire*

OTHER BOOKS BY JULIETTE DUNCAN

Find all of Juliette Duncan's books on her website:
www.julietteduncan.com/library

Billionaires with Heart Christian Romance Series

Her Kind-Hearted Billionaire

A reluctant billionaire, a grieving young woman, and the trip that changes their lives forever...

Her Generous Billionaire

A grieving billionaire, a solo mother, and a woman determined to sabotage their relationship...

Her Disgraced Billionaire

A billionaire in jail, a nurse who cares, and the challenge that changes their lives forever...

"The Billionaires with Heart Christian Romance Series" is a series of stand-alone books that are both God honoring and entertaining. Get your copy now,

enjoy and be blessed!

A Time for Everything Series

A Time For Everything Series is a mature-age contemporary Christian romance series set in Sydney, Australia and Texas, USA. If you like real-life characters, faith-filled families, and friendships that become something more, then you'll love these inspirational second-chance romances.

The True Love Series

Set in Australia, what starts out as simple love story grows into a family saga, including a dad battling bouts of depression and guilt, an ex-wife with issues of her own, and a young step-mum trying to mother a teenager who's confused and hurting. Through it all, a love story is woven. A love story between a caring God and His precious children as He gently draws them to Himself and walks with them through the trials and joys of life.

"A beautiful Christian story. I enjoyed all of the books in this series. They all brought out Christian concepts of faith in action."

"Wonderful set of books. Weaving the books from story to story. Family living, God, & learning to trust Him with all their hearts."

The Precious Love Series

The Precious Love Series continues the story of Ben, Tessa and Jayden from the The True Love Series, although each book can be read on its own. All of the books in this series will warm your heart and draw you closer to the God who loves and cherishes you without condition.

"I loved all the books by Juliette, but those about Jaydon and Angie's stories are my favorites...can't wait for the next one..."

"Juliette Duncan has earned my highest respect as a Christian romance writer. She continues to write such touching stories about real life and the tragedies, turmoils, and joys that happen while we are living. The words that she uses to write about her characters relationships with God can only come from someone that has had a very close & special with her Lord and Savior herself. I have read all of her books and if you are a reader of Christian fiction books I would highly recommend her books." Vicki

~

The Shadows Series

An inspirational romance, a story of passion and love, and of God's inexplicable desire to free people from pasts that haunt them so they can live a life full of His peace, love and forgiveness, regardless of the circumstances. Book 1, *"Lingering Shadows"* is set in England, and follows the story of Lizzy, a headstrong, impulsive young lady from a privileged background, and Daniel, a roguish Irishman who sweeps her off her feet. But can Lizzy leave the shadows of her past behind and give Daniel the love he deserves, and will Daniel find freedom and release in God?

Hank and Sarah - A Love Story, the Prequel to "The Madeleine Richards Series" is a FREE thank you gift for joining my mailing list. You'll also be the first to hear about my next books and get exclusive sneak previews. Get your free copy at www.julietteduncan.com/subscribe

The Madeleine Richards Series

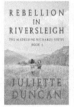  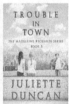 

Although the 3 book series is intended mainly for pre-teen/ Middle Grade girls, it's been read and enjoyed by people of all ages.

"Juliette has a fabulous way of bringing her characters to life. Maddy is at typical teenager with authentic views and actions that truly make it feel like you are feeling her pain and angst. You want to enter into her situation and make everything better. Mom and soon to be dad respond to her with love and gentle persuasion while maintaining their faith and trust in Jesus, whom they know, will give them wisdom as they continue on their lives journey. Appropriate for teenage readers but any age can enjoy." Amazon Reader

The Homecoming

Kayla McCormack is a famous pop-star, but her life is a mess. Dane Carmichael has a disability, but he has a heart for God. He had a crush on her at school, but she doesn't remember him. His simple faith and life fascinate her, but can she surrender her life of fame and fortune to find true love?

Unchained

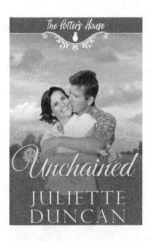

Imprisoned by greed – redeemed by love

Sally Richardson has it all. A devout, hard-working, well-respected husband, two great kids, a beautiful home, wonderful friends. Her life is perfect. Until it isn't.

When Brad Richardson, accountant, business owner, and respected church member, is sentenced to five years in jail, Sally is shell-shocked. How had she not known about her husband's fraudulent activity? And how, as an upstanding member of their tight-knit community, did he ever think he'd get away with it? He's defrauded clients, friends, and fellow church members. She doubts she can ever trust him again.

Locked up with murderers and armed robbers, Brad knows that the only way to survive his incarceration is to seek God with all his heart - something he should have done years ago. But how does he convince his family that his remorse is genuine? Will they ever forgive him?

He's failed them. But most of all, he's failed God. His poor decisions have ruined this once perfect family.

They've lost everything they once held dear. Will they lose each other as well?

Blessings of Love

She's going on mission to help others. He's going to win her heart.

Skye Matthews, bright, bubbly and a committed social work major, is the pastor's daughter. She's in love with Scott Anderson, the most eligible bachelor, not just at church, but in the entire town.

Scott lavishes her with flowers and jewellery and treats her like a lady, and Skye has no doubt that life with him would be amazing. And yet, sometimes, she can't help but feel he isn't committed enough. Not to her, but to God.

She knows how important Scott's work is to him, but she has a niggling feeling that he isn't prioritising his faith, and that concerns her. If only he'd join her on the mission trip to Burkina Faso…

Scott Anderson, a smart, handsome civil engineering graduate, has just received the promotion he's been working for for months. At age twenty-four, he's the youngest employee to ever hold a position of this calibre, and he's pumped.

Scott has been dating Skye long enough to know that she's 'the one', but just when he's about to propose, she asks him to go on mission with her. His plans of marrying her are thrown to the wind.

Can he jeopardise his career to go somewhere he's never heard of, to work amongst people he'd normally ignore?

If it's the only way to get a ring on Skye's finger, he might just risk it…

And can Skye's faith last the distance when she's confronted with a truth she never expected?

Stand Alone Christian Romantic Suspense

Leave Before He Kills You

When his face grew angry, I knew he could murder…
That face drove me and my three young daughters to flee across

Australia.

I doubted he'd ever touch the girls, but if I wanted to live and see them grow, I had to do something.

The plan my friend had proposed was daring and bold, but it also gave me hope.

My heart thumped. What if he followed?

Radical, honest and real, this Christian romantic suspense is one woman's journey to freedom you won't put down…get your copy and read it now.

ABOUT THE AUTHOR

Juliette Duncan is a Christian fiction author, passionate about writing stories that will touch her readers' hearts and make a difference in their lives. Although a trained school teacher, Juliette spent many years working alongside her husband in their own business, but is now relishing the opportunity to follow her passion for writing stories she herself would love to read. Based in Brisbane, Australia, Juliette and her husband have five adult children, eight grandchildren, and an elderly long haired dachshund. Apart from writing, Juliette loves exploring the great world we live in, and has travelled extensively, both within Australia and overseas. She also enjoys social dancing and eating out.

Connect with Juliette:

Email: juliette@julietteduncan.com

Website: www.julietteduncan.com

Facebook: www.facebook.com/JulietteDuncanAuthor

Twitter: https://twitter.com/Juliette_Duncan

Made in United States
North Haven, CT
29 September 2023

42155933R00088